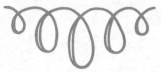

ALADDIN
NEW YORK   LONDON   TORONTO   SYDNEY   NEW DELHI

KATARINA
Ballerina

By
TILER PECK
& **KYLE HARRIS**

Illustrated by **SUMITI COLLINA**

This book is a work of fiction. Any references to historical events, real people, or real places are used fictitiously. Other names, characters, places, and events are products of the author's imagination, and any resemblance to actual events or places or persons, living or dead, is entirely coincidental.

ALADDIN
An imprint of Simon & Schuster Children's Publishing Division
1230 Avenue of the Americas, New York, New York 10020
First Aladdin hardcover edition May 2020
Text copyright © 2020 by Pecksterina & Co., Inc., and Kyle Harris
Illustrations copyright © 2020 by Sumiti Collina
All rights reserved, including the right of reproduction in whole or in part in any form.
ALADDIN and related logo are registered trademarks of Simon & Schuster, Inc.
For information about special discounts for bulk purchases, please contact
Simon & Schuster Special Sales at 1-866-506-1949 or business@simonandschuster.com.
The Simon & Schuster Speakers Bureau can bring authors to your live event. For more
information or to book an event contact the Simon & Schuster Speakers Bureau
at 1-866-248-3049 or visit our website at www.simonspeakers.com.
Book designed by Tiara Iandiorio
The illustrations for this book were rendered digitally.
The text of this book was set in Sofia Pro.
Manufactured in the United States of America 0320 FFG
10 9 8 7 6 5 4 3 2 1
Library of Congress Cataloging-in-Publication Data
Names: Peck, Tiler, author. | Harris, Kyle, 1986- author. | Collina, Sumiti, illustrator.
Title: Katarina Ballerina / by Tiler Peck & Kyle Harris ; illustrated by Sumiti Collina.
Description: First Aladdin hardcover edition. | New York, New York : Aladdin, 2020. |
Series: Katarina Ballerina ; 1 | Audience: Ages 8-12. | Audience: Grades 4-6. |
Summary: With determination and help from her new friends, a ten-year-old
New York City girl overcomes obstacles in her pursuit of becoming a prima ballerina.
Identifiers: LCCN 2019059807 (print) | LCCN 2019059808 (eBook) |
ISBN 9781534452763 (hardcover) | ISBN 9781534452787 (eBook)
Subjects: CYAC: Ballet dancing—Fiction. | Determination (Personality trait)—Fiction. |
Friendship—Fiction. | New York (N.Y.)—Fiction.
Classification: LCC PZ7.1.P43815 Kat 2020 (print) |
LCC PZ7.1.P43815 (eBook) | DDC [Fic]—dc23
LC record available at https://lccn.loc.gov/2019059807
LC eBook record available at https://lccn.loc.gov/2019059808

FOR OUR MOTHERS, OUR GRANDMOTHERS,
OUR MENTORS, OUR TEACHERS,
WHO TAUGHT US THAT OUR WORDS ARE
ONLY MATCHED BY THE POWER OF OUR DREAMS.
TO EVERYONE WHO'S EVER BEEN
AFRAID TO TAKE THE FIRST STEP.
LEAP, AND THE NET WILL APPEAR.

—T. P. AND K. H.

KATARINA Ballerina

Chapter 1

"**D**AD!" **KATARINA CRIED.** She'd been battling her hair for so long that her arms were starting to go numb from holding them over her head. No matter what she did, she couldn't get her curls under control. "I need your help!"

"Never fear, Dad is here!" he said in the deep, silly superhero voice of his that always made Katarina laugh. He squeezed into the tiny bathroom behind her and kissed the top of her head. "What's up, buttercup?"

"Can you put my hair in a ponytail?" She handed him the comb and hair tie. "A nice smooth one with no bumps on top?" That was how the other girls at school did *their* hair. Stef and Darci had started it, and now everyone wore their hair in the tightest, slickest ponytail they could manage. Too bad Katarina's cloud of curls didn't want to cooperate.

"I can try, sweetie," her dad said, getting to work. He'd gotten a lot better at doing her hair over the past couple of years. "But why not just wear it down today? You have such beautiful hair."

Katarina sighed. He would never understand. He was always telling her she was extraordinary, which was really sweet and exactly the kind of thing a good dad *should* say. But all Katarina wanted, just for once, was to fit in.

"I think that's the best I can do," he said after he'd wrestled her hair into a ponytail. It was still bumpy on top—not like the smooth, glossy

ponytails Stef and Darci wore—but it was probably as good as it was going to get. "Come on, breakfast is almost ready."

Katarina gave herself one last look in the mirror before the heavenly smell of cooking bacon made her forget her hair and sprint for the table. Her dad went back to the stove, poking at the bacon with a spatula. Their dog, Lulu, a fluffy Maltipoo with big brown eyes, was sitting at his feet, trembling with concentration as she watched his every move, hoping he'd drop one of the bacon strips.

"Oops!" he said, deliberately dropping a piece onto the floor like he always did. Lulu pounced on it, gobbling it up with glee. Katarina laughed. She liked bacon too, but Lulu loved it more than anything else in the world.

"How can you even taste it when you eat that fast, Lulu?" she asked. The dog just cocked her head and blinked up at her.

"Here you go, sweetie," her dad said as he handed her a plate containing the Dad Special: a smiley face made of two eggs over easy for eyes, a strawberry nose, and a ribbon of bacon for a smile.

"Yum!" Katarina said, diving in.

"How can you even taste it when you eat that fast?" her dad teased.

Katarina grinned and rolled her eyes. "Ha ha, very funny."

Katarina had eaten only one wobbly egg when she glanced at the clock on the stove and dropped her fork.

"Oh man!" she said. "I've got to go!" She hadn't realized how much time she'd spent doing battle with her hair.

"What's the hurry?" her dad asked. "You've still got plenty of time before school starts. You haven't even touched your mouth!" He gestured at the strip of bacon on her plate.

"I want to get there early," she said, swinging her bag onto her back and wrapping her scarf around her neck. She grabbed the piece of bacon to take with her and eat on the walk to school. "Love you! Come on, Lulu!"

"Have a good day!" her dad called after them as Katarina and Lulu dashed from the apartment.

As usual, her neighborhood of Sunnyside was humming with activity. Pigeons pecked at the sidewalk, buses rumbled along the streets,

and the smell of fresh doughnuts being made at the shop on the corner wafted through the air. Katarina waved at her neighbor Mrs. Morris, who was watering the pots of daisies on her stoop, and Lulu barked at the orange tabby cat who was always sitting in the window of the apartment across the street. It was an ordinary day, except that when she got to the end of the block, where she was supposed to turn left to head to school, Katarina turned right.

This was why Katarina had been leaving for school early. Last Saturday, when she and her dad had been walking home after picking up Indian food from their favorite restaurant, Katarina had spotted it. The electronics store on Forty-Third Street had two big-screen TVs in its windows that would play the same thing on a loop for weeks. It had been a nature documentary about whales last month, but Katarina had nearly dropped their dinner when she'd seen what the video had changed to. Ever since that night, she'd been walking two blocks out of her way every morning on her way to school in order to spend a few minutes watching.

Katarina stopped in front of the window of Electro-Land, staring at the image on one of the giant screens. Four beautiful ballerinas floated across a stage, their hands linked together as they jumped and moved in perfect unison. Their tutus looked like shimmering cotton candy, and on top of their hair—which was pulled back into the sleekest, shiniest buns Katarina had ever seen—they wore sparkling feather head-dresses. They were so strong and graceful, and more than anything Katarina wanted to be like them one day.

As she watched, she mimicked their moves. She stood as tall on her toes as she could and tried to flutter her feet when she jumped the

way the ballerinas did. She wasn't as good as they were, but she'd been practicing in secret in her room at night and she was getting better. She'd asked her dad if she could take ballet lessons about a thousand times, but he'd always said no, that lessons were expensive and they couldn't afford them. Katarina could tell it made him sad to have to tell her no, so she stopped asking and starting practicing on her own. Sometimes she danced along with lessons on YouTube, and other times she just put on a song and moved in whatever way the music made her feel. It might not be real lessons, but she was sure all the practice was paying off anyway. She'd almost broken a lamp the first time she'd tried to spin all the way around on one foot, but now she could do it without falling over. Sometimes when she closed her eyes, she could imagine herself dancing in front of a huge crowd of people. She'd leap and twirl across the stage, and everyone would jump to their feet to clap for her when she was finished!

"Coo-*coo*!"

Katarina jumped, her eyes flying open. She hadn't even realized she'd closed them, but while she'd been imagining dancing for an adoring audience, a group of pigeons had gathered on the sidewalk next to her. No doubt they were eyeing the half-eaten strip of bacon she was holding.

"Go! Shoo!" she said.

But they didn't move. The biggest and bravest one even hopped a little closer to her on his thin pink feet. Katarina looked down at the pigeon's spindly toes, which curved inward toward his body, and then down at her own. She had pigeon toes too. Whereas most people's feet pointed straight ahead, hers had always turned in a little bit, like her big toes were two magnets, always being pulled together by some invisible force. None of the perfect ballerinas in the video had toes like that.

The big pigeon squawked again, but Katarina imagined he was actually laughing at her.

You want to be a real ballerina? she imagined him saying. *Good luck when you have toes that look just like mine!*

Suddenly Lulu barked at the crowd of pigeons, scaring them away in a flurry of feathers. Katarina laughed and knelt down to hug Lulu around the neck.

"Thanks, Lu," she said. Lulu wagged her tail hopefully, and Katarina gave her the last bite of her bacon.

Katarina's watch buzzed, and she jumped up. It was the alarm she'd set to make sure she didn't accidentally watch the ballet for so long that she was late to school, like she'd done yesterday. She'd better get moving!

She used the rest of her walk to school to get in some more practice. She leapt down the sidewalk and worked on her spins while she waited at crosswalks. In her mind, she was wearing a snow-white tutu and feathers, standing with the ballerinas from the video, dancing in perfect sync with them. Someday, she was sure, she would be a real ballerina, no matter what any pesky pigeon said!

Chapter 2

KATARINA TWIRLED UP to the steps of her school as the last of the stragglers headed inside. She bent down to scratch behind Lulu's ears.

"Have a good day!" she told her. "I'll see you later."

Lulu barked and ran for Mr. Rajan's bodega on the corner. He loved her and would have a bowl of water and a dog treat waiting for her, just like every morning. Lulu would spend the school day greeting his customers with her wagging tail or snoozing on a pillow next to the refrigerator that held the sodas and bottles of water. Katarina used to try to leave Lulu at home when she went to school, but Lulu didn't like to be that far away from her and would whine and cry. Once she'd even taken a divot out of the front door, scratching to get out, so this arrangement worked better for everyone.

Katarina was out of breath from dancing all the way to school and running down the halls when she slipped into Mrs. Piskin's class just seconds before the late bell rang.

"Close one, Katarina!" Mrs. Piskin said as she closed the classroom door behind her.

"Thanks," Katarina said, panting, and went to take her seat. She sat right behind Darci and looked with envy at her ponytail as she sat down. It was so tight and sleek, slicked back into a ruffly hair tie with some kind of glitter gel that made her hair sparkle, her red tresses falling as straight as a pin halfway down her back. It was beautiful. Katarina would never be able to get her hair to look like that.

"Morning, Darci," she said. "I really love your ponytail."

Darci slowly turned in her chair to look at Katarina, and Katarina held her breath as Darci cast her eyes over Katarina's own ponytail.

"Yours is, um, nice too," she said, giving Katarina a half-hearted smile. Then Darci's eyes met Stef's from across the room, and they both started to giggle.

Katarina's heart sank. Mrs. Piskin began calling the roll, and as soon as she got to Katarina's name, Katarina shot her arm up in the air.

"Yes, Katarina?" the teacher asked.

"Can I have a bathroom pass, please?"

Mrs. Piskin frowned, because school had started only a couple of minutes ago, but she gave Katarina the pass anyway and told her to hurry back. Katarina dashed to the girls' restroom down the hall and pulled out her hair tie, letting her curls loose. She wet her hands in the sink and then used them to pull her hair back into the slickest, tightest ponytail she could manage. Her head ached a little from how tight it was, but that seemed like a small price to pay.

After long division and history, it was time for recess and lunch break. Katarina and her friends started a game of freeze tag on the playground, chasing one another up the big plastic slide, weaving around the swings, and dodging past the monkey bars. With just a few minutes of recess left, Katarina snuck away from the game. There was an old wooden balance beam between two parts of the playground structure that hardly anyone ever used, and it made a perfect barre for practicing dance moves. Katarina stood beside it, laying a palm on the faded wood and letting the other hang at her side. She put her feet into first position the way she'd learned from a ballet video on YouTube, turning her turned-in toes as far *out* as she could, making her feet into a wide V shape. She hummed the piano tune that accompanied the video and began to go through the movements she'd practically memorized by now, bending her knees and lifting her arms as gracefully as she could into the air. She imagined herself in pretty pink toe shoes with ribbons that wove up her legs, wearing a floating white tutu like the ballerinas in the video at Electro-Land, a rapt audience watching her every move.

"Whatcha doing?" a voice suddenly asked.

Katarina spun around, but she breathed a sigh of relief when she saw that it was just her friend Grant, a sandy-haired boy who always seemed to have a smile on his face, even when it was raining and he had a sniffle and he'd lost his homework. Katarina had been keeping her dancing a secret because she didn't want anyone to know about it until she was really good, but she thought it would be okay to tell Grant.

"I'm practicing my ballet," Katarina said.

"Cool!" he said. "I didn't know you took ballet lessons."

"I don't." She stood up on her toes and reached her arms above her head in an oval. "My dad says they're too expensive, but I've been teaching myself from lessons on the internet."

"Can you teach me, too?" he asked.

"Sure!" Katarina said. He put his hand on the barre next to her, and she showed him how to position his feet and move his arms.

"Wow, this is harder than it looks!" he said as he struggled to keep his balance while standing in fourth position.

"I know, but it gets easier the more you do it," she said. "And so far I've only *almost* broken one lamp trying to learn how to spin."

Grant laughed. "I broke a lamp last week playing soccer in the house!"

"I guess no lamp is safe," Katarina said.

Then Mrs. Piskin, standing at the door of the school, began ringing her big brass bell, which signaled the end of recess. Katarina and Grant, along with everyone else in their class, ran toward the door to line up for lunch. If you weren't near the front of the line, there was a chance all of the chocolate milk would be gone by the time you got through the lunch line and you'd have to settle for regular milk.

"Will you show me some more moves sometime?" Grant asked as they ran through the grass.

"You bet!" Katarina replied. She couldn't remember why she had ever wanted to keep her dancing a secret in the first place.

Katarina and Grant snagged two of the last chocolate milks and sat with the rest of their friends to eat their soggy, square slices of pizza and some mysterious lump of vegetables Katarina thought were green beans. Or maybe asparagus. Well, at least she hadn't gotten stuck with plain milk!

"Hey, where did you go during recess?" her friend Amelie asked her. "You and Grant disappeared!"

"Oh," Katarina said. Should she tell Amelie she was practicing her dancing? She felt suddenly nervous for everyone to know. "Well, um, my ring slipped off my finger while we were playing tag. Grant was helping me look for it. Right, Grant?"

"What? Oh . . . yeah!" he said. "It fell in the gravel and was practically invisible. It took us forever to find it."

Katarina gave him a grateful smile.

At the front of the cafeteria, Principal Hernandez stepped onto the small stage that overlooked all the tables. Every day at lunch he made announcements using a microphone that caused the speakers to squeal whenever he turned it on.

"Here we go," Katarina said.

"Assume your positions!" her friend Michael added.

They all put their fingers in their ears and braced for the high-pitched sound.

Squeeeeak!

Immediately the roar of kids talking and laughing died down as everyone else clapped their hands over their ears.

"Good afternoon, everyone," Principal Hernandez said. "Here are the day's announcements. The science club meeting after school has been moved from Wednesday to Thursday. A lost backpack found in the boys' bathroom on the second floor has been turned in to the office. The third-grade field trip to . . ."

Katarina's mind started to wander. There was just something about Principal Hernandez's droning voice that made him almost impossible to listen to for more than about ten seconds.

Sometimes her dad had trouble sleeping, and she thought if she could just make a recording of the principal's voice for him to listen to, he would never have that problem again.

But then Principal Hernandez said something that suddenly made him the most interesting man in the world.

"And finally, next Friday night we'll be holding our annual fall talent show," he said. "If you can sing, dance, play a musical instrument, or anything else, I invite you to come and sign up to take part. The talent show will be held in the auditorium, and this year the winner will receive a prize of one hundred dollars!"

Katarina gasped, and the cafeteria erupted with whoops and cheers. The talent show had never had a prize before! Katarina imagined herself up on the stage in the auditorium, the lights on her as she danced, and her heart started beating faster.

"A hundred dollars!" Grant said. "Do you have

any idea how much candy that would buy?"

Or maybe, Katarina thought as the idea hit her, *it could buy some real ballet lessons.*

"The sign-up sheet will be available in the front office starting tomorrow morning," Principal Hernandez continued. "I hope to see lots of you signing up!"

"Do you have a talent, Grant?" Amelie asked him.

"Hmm, not really. But for a hundred dollars I'll come up with one!" he said. "What about you?"

"My mom's been making me take piano lessons since I was six," Amelie said. "Maybe I'll play a song for the show."

"I can juggle!" Michael said, grabbing the apple off of Grant's lunch tray and the uneaten banana from his own backpack and tossing them into the air.

"Ooh, you could do a clown act!" Amelie said. "I think you'd look great with a big curly wig and some giant shoes."

"Ha ha," Michael said, grinning. "What about you, Katarina?"

This was it! This was Katarina's chance to become a dancer just like the ballerinas she watched in the Electro-Land window. She would dance in the talent show, and everyone, including her dad, would see how good she was. She'd win the grand prize, use the money to pay for real ballet lessons, and become an amazing dancer who performed for sold-out audiences every night!

Katarina smiled at the vision in her head. "I think I'll dance a ballet solo."

Amelie cocked her head at Katarina. "I didn't know you danced."

"She's been teaching herself," Grant explained. "She's pretty good."

"But . . ." Michael frowned in confusion. "Don't you have to take, like, years and years of classes to do ballet? It's not just like dancing along to music on the radio or something."

"Yeah," Amelie said. "Are you sure you want to dance in front of the whole school if you're just starting to learn how? I *never* would have played the piano in front of everyone when I was only a beginner."

Katarina's beautiful vision was dissolving before her eyes. What if Amelie and Michael were right? What if she got up and danced in front of the whole school and made a fool of herself? Practicing ballet in her room at night alongside videos on the internet wasn't *real* dance training. What if she did the talent show and everyone laughed at her? She might never feel like she fit in at school again, and the last thing she wanted was to feel like more of an outsider with her turned-in toes and curly hair. "Maybe you're right. Maybe I shouldn't," she said, her heart sinking into her stomach. "I doubt I could win anyway."

"Well, I think you should!" Grant protested. "You really love dancing, so who cares if you win or not?"

"Do you really think I should?" Katarina asked.

"Heck yeah, I do!" Grant said. "You can't sign up until tomorrow morning anyway. Promise you'll at least think about it?"

Katarina nodded. She would definitely be thinking about it, probably all day long. "I will."

Chapter 3

KATARINA HAD NO trouble keeping her promise to Grant. Not only did she think about whether or not to enter the talent show all day, but she thought about it all night, too. She tossed and turned so much that Lulu, who always spent the night at her feet, finally jumped off the bed and curled up on the carpet to get some sleep. Katarina's mind wouldn't stop racing. Grant was right that she loved ballet more than almost anything in the world, and the idea of showing everyone what she'd been working on all this time, while scary, was also really exciting. After all, if she wanted to be a real ballerina, she had to start dancing in front of people sometime, right? And if she won the prize money, she was *sure* her dad would let her start taking real ballet lessons.

But she couldn't quite shake her doubts, either. All she knew about ballet was what she'd picked up from videos on the internet and in the window at Electro-Land. What if she wasn't any good? What if her classmates made fun of her? Katarina growled and jammed her pillow over her head.

"Katarina! Time to get up!" Her dad's voice filtered through her fuzzy head and the pillow she was still buried under. She sat up and rubbed her eyes, looking at the light streaming in through her bedroom window, and wondered when she'd finally fallen asleep.

"Hey, sleepyhead," her dad said when she staggered into the kitchen. He handed her a glass of apple juice. "How'd you sleep?"

As Katarina sat down at the kitchen table and sipped her juice, she thought about the hours she'd spent debating about the talent show in her head and the dream she'd had when she finally did fall asleep. Stef and Darci had been chasing her through the halls of the school, and she'd struggled to run away from them in ballet slippers that were as big and floppy on her feet as clown shoes.

"Not great," she said.

"I'm sorry to hear that," he said. "But maybe this will cheer you up. I made your favorite, huevos rancheros!"

Katarina brightened a little. She might not know what to do about the talent show, but her dad did make the *best* huevos rancheros. Actually, practically everything he made was the best. He worked at a real estate firm, but he was always talking about how he wished he could open up a restaurant of his own instead.

Her dad handed her a brightly colored plate and then sat beside her to eat breakfast. "Are you okay, honey?" he asked. "You seem like you've been a little distracted."

Katarina sighed and speared a tomato with her fork. "I guess I have a dilemma."

"Want to tell me about it?" he asked. "Maybe I can help."

Katarina took a bite of the huevos rancheros. The eggs were fluffy and the salsa was sharp and flavorful but not too spicy. It was perfect.

"Why did you decide to become a real estate broker instead of a chef?" she asked. "That's what you really *wanted* to do, right?"

He nodded. "I even went to culinary school for a year. But, well, life got complicated. It just made more sense for me to have a regular nine-to-five job than to try to open up a restaurant like I wanted to when I was young."

"Were you scared of failing?" Katarina asked, imagining herself falling onstage as she tried to do some ballet move and all of her classmates laughing at her.

"I guess that was part of it," he said. "What's this about?"

"There's something I want to do," she said, "but I'm scared it won't go well. What if people make fun of me?"

"Do you love this thing the way I love cooking?"

She nodded.

He covered her hand with his own. "Then you should do it. I wish I had learned to follow my heart and take chances when I was your age. If something makes you happy, you should do it no matter what anyone else says. Except . . . this thing isn't illegal, is it?"

Katarina laughed. "No!"

"Just checking," he said with a grin. "Then I say go for it!"

"Okay," Katarina said, her heart feeling suddenly light. "I'm going to!"

"That's my girl," he said. "Now eat up before it gets cold."

Katarina was so happy with her decision to enter the talent show that she danced all the way to school, Lulu right on her heels. She got some strange looks as she skipped and twirled her way down the sidewalks, but she didn't care what anyone else thought. She loved dancing, so she was going to do it! She gave Lulu a kiss goodbye at the corner by Mr. Rajan's bodega and then practiced her leaps—which ballet dancers called "jetés"—all the way into the school. She pushed open the door to the front office and pirouetted her way inside, stopping only when she reached the desk.

"Good morning, Miss Chen!" she said to the secretary. "I'm here to sign up for the talent show!"

"Well, I can see that!" Miss Chen said,

sliding the clipboard with the talent show sign-up list toward her. "I'm guessing you'll be dancing for us?"

"That's right!" Katarina said, writing her name down on the list. "I'm going to do a ballet solo."

"I look forward to seeing it, dear," Miss Chen said. "Now, you'd better dance off to class before the bell rings!"

Normally Katarina liked school, but she couldn't wait for the day to be over so that she could get home and start working. She'd never put together an actual dance routine before; she'd always just followed along with ballet videos or danced however the music she was listening to made her feel. But she knew that wouldn't work for the talent show. She needed to have a dance memorized, which meant picking a song and choreographing a routine. She struggled to pay attention to the lessons Mrs. Piskin was teaching because ideas for her routine kept running through her head, and her toes kept dancing underneath her desk no matter how hard she tried to stop them.

"So, I decided I'm going to do the talent show," she told her friends as they sat down in the cafeteria for lunch.

"That's awesome!" Grant said, grinning. "You're going to do great. I just know it."

"You think?" Katarina asked. "I'm excited, but I'm still pretty nervous, too."

"Yeah, you'll be amazing," Amelie said.

"But I haven't taken lots of real ballet classes or anything," Katarina said, remembering what Amelie had said the day before.

Michael shrugged. "Who cares about that? I haven't taken any juggling classes, but I'm still going to win that grand prize."

"Ha!" Amelie said. "That's what *you* think. You'll have to come through me to get it!"

"And me!" Katarina added.

"Me too!" Grant chimed in.

"Did you even come up with a talent yet?" Michael asked.

"Nope, but when I do, it's going to be great!" he said, and they all laughed.

As soon as school was over, Katarina and Lulu ran home so Katarina could get started on her dance routine. The talent show was the next Friday, and there was no time to waste if she wanted to win that prize!

The first thing she needed to do was pick a piece of music to dance to. Katarina had dozens of YouTube videos of beautiful ballet dances saved on her iPad, and she started scrolling through them, looking for just the right piece of music. After a little too long watching other ballerinas dance, she realized she'd known her perfect song all along: "Waltz of the Flowers." Her mom had always played and hummed it, and it was a special song for both of them. Her mom had loved dancing to it as well. Having a little reminder of her mom with her during the show made Katarina smile. Plus, the song made her feet itch to dance, which she figured was a good sign!

Her dad wouldn't be home for at least another hour, so Katarina played the song at top volume and began to dance along. At first she just moved however the music made her feel, twirling up high on her toes when the music sounded light and joyful, moving her arms gracefully, like she was painting a big, beautiful picture. She spun with the beat of the music. Lulu even joined in, prancing around at Katarina's feet as she danced. Slowly, Katarina began to create a routine made up of her own moves and things she had learned from watching ballet videos online.

She was doing a spin when she caught sight of herself in the mirror that hung on the door of her closet. She frowned at the image looking back at her. *That* person didn't look like a real ballerina at all! She was wearing a striped hoodie and scuffed sneakers and had a wild cloud of curls around her face. The next thing Katarina needed was a costume.

Luckily, she was surrounded by inspiration. For months she'd been collecting pictures of ballerinas from magazines and getting her dad to print her favorite images off the internet at his office. There were dozens of paper ballerinas stuck to the walls of her bedroom, and she studied them. They were all a little different, but most of them had the same costume pieces in common: a leotard, a tutu, and toe shoes tied with ribbons.

Of course, Katarina didn't have any of those things. But she was pretty sure she could make something just like them!

Taking a deep breath and bracing herself, Katarina threw open the door of her closet and a small avalanche of clothes and belongings came tumbling out. She knew, somewhere in all of this, she had a red swimsuit that had sleeves. She'd gotten it last summer to take swimming lessons at the YMCA. The suit would make a great leotard for her ballet costume. All she had to do . . . was find it.

Katarina began combing through the pile. Lulu helped, digging through the clothes with her paws.

"Maybe Dad's right," Katarina told Lulu.

"Maybe it *isn't* a good idea to just shove things into my closet whenever he tells me to clean my room."

Lulu barked.

"Ooh!" Katarina said, spotting something. It wasn't the swimsuit, though. It was a pair of pink shoes that she wore sometimes when she needed to dress up in a nice outfit. If she squinted at them, they almost looked like a ballerina's pointe shoes. All they needed were ribbons. . . .

There! Hanging above her head was a dress she hadn't worn in ages, and it had a pink satin ribbon that went around the waist. The pink shoes and the satin ribbon, with the help of some scissors and thread, would make the perfect ballet slippers.

Katarina dug a bit more. She'd kind of forgotten what was in her closet! As she moved over an old soccer ball, she saw a box in the back. Curious, she grabbed the box, carefully lifting the lid and pushing aside some tissue paper.

Nestled in the wrapping was a pair of old, worn toe shoes. The ribbons were frayed, and the shoes were scuffed from lots of use. Katarina gingerly took out one shoe, holding it in the palms of her hands. She saw two initials in the back of the shoe.

They were her mother's.

For a second, Katarina couldn't believe it. She didn't even know that her dad had hung on to them. And how did they get in the back of her closet?

Maybe it was a sign that she was on the right track.

After putting the shoes back—carefully, on a shelf this time—Katarina renewed her search, even more determined than ever to create her look.

Finally, under a box of old Nancy Drew books, Katarina found her red swimsuit. It would make a perfect leotard.

All that was left was the tutu—the hardest part. As much junk as there was in her closet, Katarina knew there was no tutu hidden in there.

She had to get creative.

Katarina wandered from room to room, looking for anything she could make into a tutu.

"What about this?" she said to Lulu as they searched the bathroom, grabbing the fluffy blue loofah from its hook in the shower. "It kind of looks like a tutu, doesn't it?"

Lulu just stared back at her.

"Except it's really small," Katarina said, her heart sinking. "I'd need, like, a hundred of them to make a tutu big enough for me to wear. Let's keep looking."

There was nothing promising in the rest of the bathroom or the living room. She found one possibility in the kitchen—a box of coffee filters—but although they were frilly and stiff like a tutu, they presented the same problem as the loofah. She'd need a *lot* of them to make something she could actually wear. Katarina decided to put the problem of the tutu aside for a little while. She was sure she'd figure something out before next Friday.

Instead, she got the tiny sewing kit down from the top shelf of the linen closet. Time to make her ballet slippers. She cut the thick satin ribbon from her old dress into four thinner ribbons. Then she sewed them to the sides of her pink shoes, crisscrossed the ribbons up her feet and ankles, and tied them in a bow, just the way the ballerinas in the pictures on her walls had done. She stood up and looked at herself in the mirror.

"Wow, Lulu!" she said, stretching one foot out in front of her and pointing her toe. "I look just like a real ballerina!"

Chapter 4

KATARINA WORKED EVERY day on her dance routine for the talent show. She told her dad about the show so he could be sure to be there, but she wouldn't tell him what she'd be performing. She wanted to see the look on his face when she surprised everyone with her ballet skills.

The weekend before the talent show, Katarina and her dad went to her baby cousin's birthday party in Brooklyn. As Katarina was wrapping the teddy bear they'd bought for her in tissue paper before putting it in the sparkly pink gift bag they'd take to the party, inspiration hit her.

"Lulu," she whispered so her dad, who was just in the other room, wouldn't overhear. "Look at this tissue paper!" She folded the light, crinkly paper like an accordion and held it to her waist. She jumped up and down a few times and the paper fluttered prettily. "If I could get a lot of this, it would make a pretty good tutu, wouldn't it?"

When she'd finished wrapping the gift, she hid the rest of the tissue paper in her bedroom. And after her cousin had opened all of her presents, leaving bows and wrapping paper strewn across the apartment, Katarina walked around picking up every sheet of tissue paper.

"Thank you, Katarina!" her aunt Marie said. "You're so sweet to help clean up."

"Oh, uh, you bet!" Katarina replied. She happily took the trash bag Aunt Marie handed her. Cleaning up the mess was a small price to pay for getting all the tutu materials she needed! While she tossed the wrapping paper and rib-bons into the trash bag, she picked up the tissue paper she collected, carefully straightened out the wrinkles, folded it neatly, and stashed it in her bag.

When she got home, she cut the elastic waistband off of an old Halloween costume she'd never wear again, borrowed her dad's stapler, and began accordion folding the pieces of tissue paper she'd found. There were a dozen pieces of paper, and when she'd stapled them all to the elastic, she had a beautiful pink, shimmery tutu that she was sure looked as good as any costume a profes-sional ballerina had ever worn. She couldn't wait for the talent show.

And she didn't have to wait long. The days seemed to fly by until the day of the talent show suddenly arrived!

Katarina tried to pay attention in school that

day, but she was so nervous and excited that she couldn't think about anything other than the talent show. When it was her turn to read her book report on *Charlotte's Web* for the class, she accidentally started to read her history paper on how the Eiffel Tower was built instead. Then at lunch she grabbed what she *thought* was an apple out of the lunchbox her dad had packed for her. She bit into it, realizing only once she was chewing that it was actually an orange. She spit out the bitter mouthful of orange peel, and her friends laughed.

"Are you a little distracted, Katarina?" Amelie asked.

Katarina laughed too. "Just a little."

The four hours between when classes let out and when she headed back to the school were torture. She tried to practice but ended up just pacing the apartment until it was time for her and her dad to leave.

"So, are you ready for your performance?"

her dad asked as they walked up the front steps of the school, Katarina carefully carrying her ballet costume in a large plastic bag.

"I think so!" Katarina said. It felt eerie being in the school after hours, with only the light from the streetlamps coming in through the windows.

"Are you going to tell me what you're planning to do now?" he asked as they made their way to the auditorium, where they heard the hum of a crowd.

"Nope!" she said. "I told you, it's going to be a surprise. I'd better go backstage and start getting ready."

"All right." He bent down and kissed the top of her head. "Break a leg, sweetie."

"What?" Katarina asked. Why would her own father say something like that to her?

But her dad just laughed. "Sorry! It means 'good luck.'"

"Ohhh, okay," she said, giving him a quick hug. "See you after the show!"

 47

Katarina ran back to the choir room, which was where all the students participating in the talent show were supposed to get ready to perform. She spotted Amelie and Michael sitting by the window. Amelie was looking over the sheet music for the piano piece she was going to play, and Michael had a box filled with objects to juggle: balls, apples, and even four delicious-looking chocolate doughnuts with rainbow sprinkles.

"They look so good," Michael was saying when she walked up. "And I'm so hungry. . . ."

"But you won't have anything to juggle for your grand finale if you eat them!" Amelie replied.

"I could just eat *one*, though, right?"

"Hey, guys!" Katarina said, sitting down beside them. "Where's Grant?"

"In the audience," Amelie said. "He never did figure out what he wanted to do for his talent."

"I thought he was going to do a magic

act?" Katarina asked. Grant had told her all about it at recess the day before.

"His sister wouldn't let him borrow her pet rabbit," Michael explained before he took a huge bite out of one of the doughnuts.

"You ready to dance, Katarina?" Amelie asked.

"Almost!" Katarina had given the recording of her music to Mrs. Murphy, who was in charge of the talent show, that morning, and she was wearing her swimsuit/leotard under her clothes. She took them off and pulled on her ballet shoes and tissue-paper tutu.

"Ooh, that's so pretty!" Amelie said, admiring the colored skirt.

"Thanks!" Katarina said. "I made it myself."

"Okay, kids!" Mrs. Murphy appeared in the doorway of the choir room. "It's time to start!"

One by one, kids left the choir room to go perform on the stage of the auditorium. When it was Amelie's turn, Katarina and Michael snuck into the theater's wings to watch. Amelie walked confidently out onto the stage, sat down at the piano bench, cracked her knuckles once, and then started to play. She was great! Her fingers flew over the keys, never missing a note. Amelie would be stiff competition for that prize money.

Michael went out next. He juggled the balls and then the apples perfectly, not dropping a single one. Then it was time for his grand finale—juggling the doughnuts—but he'd been munching on them all night and there was only one and a half left. The audience laughed when he told them what had happened, and they applauded when he juggled the one and a half doughnuts with one hand held behind his back. Katarina felt a little less nervous after watching him. At least she hadn't eaten her tutu!

Then Mrs. Murphy was announcing Katarina. This was it! She took a deep breath, walked out onto the stage, and looked out at the audience . . .

. . . and the rows and rows and *rows* of faces staring back at her. There were so many more people than she'd expected! Had the auditorium always been so gigantic? It seemed at least ten times bigger than she remembered it. She loved dancing alone in her room, imagining a huge audience watching her, but it turned out real audiences were much scarier!

A wave of nervousness crashed over Katarina like a tidal wave. She looked for the reassuring faces of her dad and Grant but couldn't find them in the crowd, and then suddenly her music was playing over the speakers. It was time to dance, but she couldn't remember a single step she'd practiced! Her mind had gone completely blank.

But then she recognized the high violin notes where she normally spun. She did the spin, tottering a little, and her memory came back. She performed the moves she'd memorized, but everything felt a little off. Her jumps

weren't as high, her arms weren't as graceful, and she was so busy worrying about all
the people watching her and what they were
thinking that she couldn't lose herself in the
music the way she usually did. She couldn't

wait for the song to be over so she could get off that stage.

She made it through the dance, and though everyone clapped when she was done, Katarina was so disappointed that she felt like she might cry. She rushed off the stage, blinking to keep the tears at bay. That hadn't even been close to the triumphant debut of her ballet skills that she'd dreamed about! There was no way she'd win first place and the prize money that came with it.

"How do you think you did?" Amelie asked when Katarina threw herself down in a chair in the choir room. She had watched from behind the curtain with Michael.

"Terrible," Katarina said.

"You didn't fall down," Michael said.

"No, but I totally froze up," Katarina said.

"Aww, it wasn't as bad as you think!" Amelie said, rubbing her shoulders comfortingly.

"Yeah, I bet no one else even noticed you

messed up," Michael said. "Hey, do you want my last doughnut? That would make me feel better if I were you."

As miserable as she was, that still made Katarina smile.

"Yeah, thanks," she said, taking the doughnut Michael handed her. She took a big bite, and the taste of chocolate, sugar, and rainbow sprinkles *did* make her feel a little better. "I guess it could have gone worse."

"Yeah, and it was only your first time dancing in front of people!" Amelie added. "Next time you come over to my house, I'll show you the video from my first piano recital. That will make you feel way better than any doughnut, because I was *terrible*."

"Really?" Katarina asked. "But you're such an amazing player."

"I am *now*," Amelie said. "I've been practicing for five years! But during that first recital, I think I played more wrong notes than right ones. No one's great at something hard the first time they try it."

"I don't know about that," Michael said in a grand voice, turning his nose up in the air. "I was born the *world's greatest* juggler!"

The girls laughed. Katarina already felt way better than when she'd come off the stage, because what Amelie said made perfect sense (and because that doughnut was delicious). She may not have danced perfectly, the way she always did when she imagined it, but it had been pretty good for her first try! If she kept practicing, in five years she could be as great at ballet as Amelie was at playing the piano.

Soon it was time to award the prizes, and Mrs. Murphy brought all of the kids back onto the stage for the announcement. She asked the audience to give them all one last round of applause before she announced the winners, and even over all of the clapping and cheering, Katarina heard her dad's whistle. When she spotted him in the crowd, he gave her two big thumbs-up, and she waved back.

"Wonderful job, everyone!" Mrs. Murphy said. "As far as I'm concerned, you're *all* winners. Now, for the judges' decisions . . ."

Katarina took Amelie's and Michael's hands.

"In third place"—Mrs. Murphy looked down at the notecard in her hand—"we have Kayla McConnell and her gymnastics routine!"

They all clapped as Kayla did a cartwheel up to Mrs. Murphy and took the small trophy she handed her.

"And in second place . . ."

Katarina held her breath as Mrs. Murphy checked her card.

"Amelie Reyes on the piano!"

Beside her, Amelie gasped. Katarina and Michael clapped wildly for Amelie as she went up to accept her trophy. Katarina even tried to do her dad's patented whistle, but she hadn't mastered it yet, so instead she just cheered.

Then it was time for Mrs. Murphy to announce the winner of the talent show. Katarina didn't really think she would win after the way her dance had gone, but she couldn't stop herself from hoping. Her heart beat faster in her chest as Mrs. Murphy got ready to read out the name, and she accidentally squeezed Michael's hand so hard that he said, "Ow!" under his breath.

"And the winner of the talent show and the one-hundred-dollar grand prize is . . ."

Kat-a-ri-na, Kat-a-ri-na . . .

"Cody Johnson singing 'Feeling Good'!"

Katarina slowly exhaled the breath she'd been holding. Well, that was that. She hadn't won the talent show, and she wouldn't be able to use the prize money to pay for real ballet lessons.

But when she met up with her dad in the hallway after the show, she was surprised that he swept her up into a giant hug, swinging her so that her feet came off the ground.

"Katarina, you were fantastic!" he said. "And

look at that tutu! A Katarina original."

"No, I wasn't," she said with a sigh. "I got so scared I forgot all my moves, and I didn't even place. I really wanted to surprise you with how good I've gotten, but nothing went the way it was supposed to."

"Oh, honey," he said. "I thought you were beautiful up there. I was so impressed. I had no idea you could dance like that!"

"I've been practicing on my own for months," she explained. "I wanted to win so I could use the prize money to take some real lessons. Oh well. I guess I'll just keep practicing and maybe I'll win next year."

Her dad was quiet for a second as they walked toward home and then said, "You really love ballet, huh?"

Katarina nodded. "More than anything in the world. Except for you and Lulu, of course."

"And you've worked so hard at it," he said. "Just like your mom." Suddenly he stopped walking and turned to face her. "Okay, you can take lessons."

Katarina froze. "What?"

"We'll sign you up for ballet lessons tomorrow," he said. "You love it, and you're really talented. You deserve it."

"But I thought we couldn't afford it?" Katarina asked.

"You let me figure that part out," her dad said. "What do you say? You still want to take lessons?"

Katarina could hardly believe her ears. She leapt into her dad's arms and hugged him tightly around the neck. "I say yes!"

Chapter 5

*T*HE NEXT DAY, just like he'd promised, Katarina's dad called around
and found a ballet studio that had an
open spot in one of their classes. The woman
on the phone told him that the other dancers in
the class had been doing ballet for a while, but
Katarina had been practicing too, even if it was
just alone in her bedroom, so Katarina was sure
it would be okay.

Katarina was so excited for her first class
that she practically floated down the side-

walk as she, her dad, and Lulu walked to the subway. Her new ballet school was across the East River in Manhattan, which made it seem even cooler and more official. Manhattan was home to the New York City Ballet, the American Ballet Theatre, Alvin Ailey, the Dance Theatre of Harlem, and many more, and these were some of the best dance companies in the world! And now it was home to Katarina's ballet school too. She was practically a real ballerina already.

Katarina and her dad swiped their MetroCards, and Katarina scooped Lulu up and put her in the shallow tote bag they used whenever they needed to take her on the subway. The three of them jumped onto the 7 train just seconds before the doors closed and it rumbled away from the platform. In her other bag, Katarina carried her tissue-paper tutu and the new pink ballet slippers her dad had bought for her after he'd signed her up for the lessons. Katarina had been wearing them around the house all week.

The train car was crowded, all the seats already taken, so they grabbed one of the silver poles that ran from the floor to the ceiling and held on as the train shook and swayed down the tracks.

As they crossed aboveground toward Manhattan, Katarina gazed out the window as the big Manhattan skyline came into view. Even though she had seen the view a gazillion times, this time felt *different*. She could feel the dreams of all the dancers who had walked between those big skyscrapers and danced on some of the world's biggest stages in this city. And she hoped she would be joining them one day.

Somewhere in the car an upbeat song with lots of intricate drumbeats was playing, and Katarina's toes began tapping. When lots of people got off at the next stop, she was able to see where the music was coming from.

At the other end of the car, a young man

dressed in colorful clothes was playing the song. He held a guitar in his arms, and around his neck he was wearing a metal frame that held a harmonica up to his lips. On his back he wore a collection of drums and cymbals of all different sizes, which were connected to other parts of his body. When he kicked his left foot, the big drum thumped. When he moved his right elbow, the cymbal crashed. The man's entire body was working to make the music, and it was the most fascinating thing Katarina had ever seen.

"Wow," she breathed, watching the man play.

"That's pretty neat," her dad said. "Want to go stand closer and watch?"

"Yeah!"

They carefully moved from pole to pole down the train car until they were standing right in front of the man. He had a hat on the ground in front of him, which contained a few bills and change, and Katarina's dad gave her a dollar to drop in it. The man flashed her a dazzling smile in between riffs on the harmonica.

When the song was over, most of the train car continued ignoring the man, but Katarina clapped wildly.

"That was amazing!" she told the man. "How did you learn to do that?"

He smiled. "Lots and lots of hard work. So, what's your name? I ride this train most of the day and I don't think I've ever seen you on it before."

"I'm Katarina," she said. "And this is my dad and my dog, Lulu. I'm going into the city to take my first ballet class."

The young man scratched Lulu's ears and held out his hand to Katarina. "Nice to meet you, Katarina. I'm Beatz."

Katarina gave his hand a shake. "That's a cool name!"

Beatz leaned down close to her and whispered, "Actually, my real name is Harold. Harold Beatman. But Beatz sounds cooler, don't you think?"

She laughed. "Definitely."

Beatz began to play another song, and Katarina and her dad listened until the train reached their stop. They waved goodbye to Beatz as they exited, the sound of his drumming following them until it was drowned out by the hustle-and-bustle noises of the city.

The ballet studio was only a couple of blocks from the subway station. Katarina's heart seemed to beat a little faster with each step they took toward it.

"Want me to go in with you?" her dad asked when they reached the little gray building with the sign that said BALLET ACADEMY EAST in fancy script.

Katarina shook her head. She didn't think the other girls would have their parents escorting them inside. "No. I'm okay."

"And you're fine to get home on your own?" he asked. "Because Lulu and I can hang around until you're done."

"It's okay," she said. "It's an easy trip, and I'm going to have to get used to doing it on my own anyway."

"Do you have your phone in case you need to get in touch with me?"

She nodded. "It's in my bag."

"Okay, this is it, then." He bent down to give her a kiss and took Lulu's leash. "Good luck, honey. Have fun!"

"I will!" Katarina said. She was finally starting ballet classes; how could it be anything *but* fun?

Katarina went inside, where a friendly woman behind the front desk pointed her to a restroom where she could change. She already had her red swimsuit on under her clothes, but she needed to put on her tutu and ballet slippers before class. Once she'd changed, Katarina did a single spin in front

of the restroom mirror, admiring the way her tutu floated on the air.

She couldn't control the grin on her face as she climbed the narrow staircase to the studio on the second floor. The walls were lined with black-and-white photographs of great ballerinas, and each picture was signed by the dancer herself. Katarina imagined being one of those ballerinas someday, surrounded by loving fans begging for her autograph. . . .

Then she stepped into the ballet studio, and all of her fantasies instantly disappeared like popped soap bubbles.

There were about a dozen girls and a few boys already in the room, stretching their muscles or chatting in small groups. They all turned and stared at her when Katarina walked in. Not only was she a stranger, but she didn't exactly fit in. The girls—who had their hair slicked back into tight buns that would make even Stef and Darci jealous—were all wearing plain black leotards and pink tights with their ballet slippers, while the three boys were wearing white shirts and black tights. Katarina, in her bright red swimsuit and rainbow-paper tutu, looked ridiculous standing with all of them. It seemed her dad hadn't gotten the memo about the uniform. Some of the other dancers whispered to one another and snickered behind their hands, and Katarina felt her cheeks getting hot.

A tall blond girl stretching at the barre near her looked Katarina up and down and arched an eyebrow at her. "Are you . . . sure you're in the right room?" she asked.

Katarina felt like she was shriveling and shrinking until she was about two feet tall. Her throat was so dry she had to swallow twice before she could speak. "This is the ballet class, right?"

Just then an older woman dressed all in black, whose silver hair was swept up in a French twist,

walked into the room. She was followed by the tiniest brown dog Katarina had ever seen, who immediately curled up by the piano in the corner and went to sleep. The woman clapped her hands, and the room fell silent.

"All right, ladies and gentlemen," she said in a thick Russian accent. "Time to dance!"

The other kids in the class immediately took their places at the barre that lined the walls of the room. Katarina didn't know what to do, so she just stood there, feeling uncertain. The woman spotted her.

"You must be Katarina," she said. "I'm Madame Alla. This is your first class, yes?"

Katarina nodded.

"Everyone, welcome Katarina," Madame Alla said to the class as she escorted Katarina to an open spot at the barre. "I expect you to be kind and helpful since she is new here."

"What, on this *planet*?" the blond ballerina who'd spoken to Katarina earlier whispered to another girl. The two of them giggled until Madame Alla gave them a sharp look. Katarina wanted to just melt through the floor and disappear.

"Hey, don't pay attention to them," the girl standing beside Katarina said with a dramatic roll of her eyes. "Honestly, they're probably just jealous. Your tutu's awesome, and these uniforms we have to wear are soooo boring."

Katarina gave her a little smile. At least there was one nice person here. "Thanks."

"Mr. Simeone, music please!" Madame Alla said.

The man sitting at the piano bench began to play.

"And two demi pliés and one grand in first, second, fourth, and fifth positions," Madame Alla called out.

This was obviously an exercise the class always did, but it was different from the one Katarina had learned from a YouTube video. She tried to follow along, but every time the group moved to the next exercise, it took her a couple of beats to catch up. She felt like she was running on a treadmill that just kept getting faster and faster and any second she'd go flying off of it.

"We're about to do grand pliés in fifth," the girl beside her whispered.

Katarina knew grand pliés were deep knee bends, but she still got the different positions mixed up. "Um . . . which one's fifth again?"

"Your legs are crossed, right in front of left, toes turned out so they kind of meet the other heel."

"Oh, right!" Katarina said, suddenly remembering. When everyone else switched positions, she was able to move with them. "Thanks!"

By the time barre was over, Katarina's legs already felt a little wobbly and weak beneath her. This class was a lot harder than dancing alone in her bedroom, and they hadn't even gotten to the actual dancing yet!

"All right, class, let's move into center." Madame Alla had them come to the middle of the floor, facing the huge mirror at the front of the room. While everyone else blended together, Katarina stuck out like a sore thumb. She tried not to look at her own reflection too much as Madame Alla began to teach them a combination of steps.

"Let's start out with something simple," she said. "We are starting in fifth position croisé. Two tendus to the front, two tendus to the back, then three tendus to the side, changing legs, and a demi plié straighten. Left side."

Everyone else in the class nodded like they understood perfectly. For a second Katarina thought maybe there was something wrong with her ears. She could tell Madame Alla was speaking some French, but it was not like the French she was learning at school. Was it? Or was Katarina not hearing right?

"Mr. Simeone!" Madame Alla said. He immediately began to play a jaunty little song, and she counted off. The dancers began their tendus in perfect unison. Every time they changed their tendu direction, their port de bras—their arm movements—changed as well.

The combination of the port de bras and the perfect, sharp leg movements was unlike anything Katarina had ever seen. They made it look so *easy*. Katarina tried to follow along, but she had no idea what she was doing, and her colorful costume in the mirror just made her flailing all the more obvious.

"No, no, no!" Madame Alla said, waving at Mr. Simeone to stop playing. Katarina froze, afraid she was about to be pointed out as the disaster she was in front of everybody (not that they couldn't already see it for themselves). But Madame Alla didn't even look at her as she continued. "It is all wrong. Where is the *aplomb*? Where are the straight legs and pointed toes? Where are my pretty fingers and pretty feet? Celeste, please show us."

The blond ballerina from earlier, who was wearing a confident smirk, took a step forward. Mr. Simeone played, and she demonstrated the combination by herself. Katarina's mouth dropped open. She might not be very nice, but she was the most beautiful dancer Katarina had ever seen.

"Now, let us try it again," Madame Alla said.

Katarina struggled through the rest of the class, trying to keep up with the others and failing miserably. What she'd thought would be one of the best days of her life had become one of the worst. She'd been kidding herself to think she could do this. She had half a mind to just throw away the stupid paper tutu and quit before she embarrassed herself even more.

Finally, mercifully, the class was over. As the other dancers grabbed their bags and began to stream out of the studio, Madame Alla placed a hand on Katarina's shoulder.

"I know today was hard," she said. "You have much to learn. But the next class will be easier."

It wasn't exactly the most encouraging speech, but Katarina did feel a *little* better. She turned to leave and found the girl who'd complimented her tutu waiting for her by the door.

"Hi," she said. "Katarina, right?"

Katarina nodded. "Yeah."

"I'm Sunny Kapoor," she said. "Are you totally miserable after that class?"

Katarina couldn't help but laugh. "A little. Is it that obvious?"

"Kind of," she admitted. "So . . . do you want some help?"

Chapter 6

*A*FTER SUCH A disastrous first ballet class, Katarina was so grateful for Sunny's offer of help that she hugged the girl right then and there. As she hugged Sunny, Katarina glanced up and saw a surprise: her dad!

"Hi, honey," her dad said, grinning. "How did my favorite ballerina do today?" He walked over and gave her a big hug.

Katarina sighed. "Not too great?"

Dad ruffled her hair. "The first class is always

going to be the hardest one. I'm sure it will be better the next time!"

That's what Madame Alla said. Katarina wasn't so sure about that. Suddenly, she remembered Sunny was still waiting.

"Oh, Dad, this is Sunny. Sunny, this is my dad," Katarina said. "Sunny promised she would help me with . . . everything! I'm a mess."

Sunny laughed. "Oh, you're not that bad! You just need a few pointers. First of all, *this*"—she waved at Katarina's homemade dance outfit—"is cool and all, but it's got to go."

Katarina nodded. "Definitely."

"Okay, my prima ballerina," Katarina's dad said. "I decided to stick around to do some work in the area and figured you could use a treat after your first class. Sunny, do you want to join us?"

"Yes!" Sunny said. Katarina smiled. Between Sunny and her dad, she was already feeling a teensy bit better. As they walked down the street, Katarina spotted a big dance clothing display in the window of a store: Happy Feet. It looked like it had all kinds of dance shoes and rows of colorful leotards hanging up.

Katarina looked at her dad. "Dad, can we just go in to look?" she asked.

Her dad hesitated but nodded. "Sure. Let's see what's in here. It sounds like you might need some more dance attire, don't you?"

As they went inside, Katarina and Sunny started looking through the leotards in the front of the store.

A nice-looking sales associate came out from the back. "Can I help you?"

"My daughter needs some more things for her ballet class," Katarina's dad explained. With Sunny's help, Katarina picked out a basic black leotard and pink tights just like the ones all the other girls in Madame Alla's class wore. Now at least Katarina would *look* the part. They took the items up to the register.

"Dad, are you sure this is okay?" Katarina asked quietly.

Her dad gave her a small smile. "Don't worry about it, Katarina. You just worry about having fun and learning in your new class." He gave her a kiss on the head and handed her the bag.

"I'd better start heading home," Sunny said. "My parents will worry if I'm late."

"Where do you live?" Katarina asked.

"Queens."

Katarina's eyes lit up. "Me too! We can ride the subway together!"

"Perfect!" Sunny said.

They walked to the nearby subway station, Katarina's dad a few steps behind, and Katarina peppered Sunny with questions all along the way.

"I didn't understand so much of what Madame Alla was saying," Katarina said. "I know a lot was French . . . but was she speaking Russian, too?"

Sunny shook her head. "Just French. Most

ballet we do today was originally developed in France, and we still use the French terms for most things."

Katarina sighed. "How am I ever going to learn all that? I thought all I needed to catch up on was dancing technique, but now I have to learn a whole new *language*?"

"I'll help you. And you don't have to learn the *whole* language," Sunny said. "All I know how to say in French other than ballet stuff is *'je suis le pamplemousse.'*"

"Wow," Katarina said, impressed. "What does that mean?"

Sunny grinned. "'I am the grapefruit.'"

Katarina burst into laughter.

"I know it wouldn't be very helpful if I ever went to France," Sunny said, "but I like the way it sounds!"

They descended the stairs to the subway platform and got onto the next train that pulled into the station. Katarina and Sunny were so busy chatting that it took Katarina a second to realize she was tapping her toe along to the sound of music.

"I wonder if that's . . ." She craned her neck, trying to look around the people crowding the train car. Then she spotted him. "It's Beatz!"

"Who?"

Katarina grabbed Sunny's hand and pulled her along down the car until they were standing in front of Beatz, who was playing a song on his musical contraption.

"That's so cool," Sunny whispered as Beatz strummed his guitar, blew into his harmonica, and jerked his arms and legs to play his drums all at once.

When the song was over, Beatz smiled at the girls. "Hey, it's Katarina the ballerina! And Katarina's friend! How was your first class?"

"It was kind of a disaster," Katarina said, "but that's okay. This is Sunny. She's a dancer too. And my dad is sitting right over there." Her dad waved from his seat.

"Nice to meet you, Sunny," Beatz said, then waved to Katarina's dad. "Now, let me see your dance moves!"

Beatz began to play another song, and Katarina and Sunny danced along with his music. It was so much fun that Katarina forgot all about the terrible dance class.

After that day, Katarina and Sunny became inseparable. Sunny lived in Long Island City, just a couple of subway stops from Katarina. On days when they didn't have ballet class, they would often meet at the park after school to play with Lulu or go over to each other's houses to spend the night on the weekends. Sunny made her a ballet dictionary of the French terms she'd need to know and quizzed her on them, and she taught Katarina the warm-up Madame Alla always did with her class. They also traveled to and from Manhattan together whenever they did have ballet class. Most days Beatz was on the train too, and they'd dance together while he played his instruments. Katarina loved her school friends like Amelie and Grant, but it was great having a new friend who liked the same things she did.

Madame Alla's class was still hard for Katarina, though. Even with Sunny helping her to catch up, she had a long way to go until she knew as much as the other dancers. Now that she had the right uniform, her clothing blended in, but she still stood out because her technique wasn't as good as everyone else's. But it didn't bother Katarina as much as it would have before because she and Sunny were having so much fun together.

"For the last combination in class, please pay attention," Madame Alla said one day. "Four piqué turns and a tombé pas de bourrée glissade jeté across the floor."

"Did she say 'pamplemousse'?" Sunny whispered to Katarina. Katarina laughed out loud, and then clapped her hand over her mouth in horror when she realized what she'd done. Madame Alla was looking at her sternly in the mirror, and beside her Sunny was turning red in the face as she tried not to laugh too.

Madame Alla clapped her hands. "Line up!"

The dancers all congregated in one corner of the studio. Katarina and Sunny made sure to stand next to each other.

"Sorry about that," Sunny said to her quietly.

Katarina gave her a look. "No, you're not."

"You're right." Sunny grinned. "It was too funny for me to be sorry."

Katarina gave her a little shove as the dancers, one by one, started doing their turns and the combination across the length of the dance floor.

"Hey, did your dad say it was okay for you to come over this weekend?" Sunny asked. "The movie theater near my house is showing *Leap!* and you *have* to see it."

"Yeah, I can't wait," Katarina said.

Celeste, who was standing right in front of Katarina, began to do her combination across the floor. Of course Celeste's was the best, gliding and moving across the floor all with the most grace and perfect extension and line. But Katarina had the chance to admire only a little of Celeste's moves before it was her turn to start going across the floor. Just a few feet behind Celeste, she began to do her best turns, trying to mimic the other girl's grace and power. But then Celeste stopped leaping. Katarina had already jumped, and there was nothing she could do but watch as she went crashing into Celeste and both of them tumbled to the floor.

"What are you doing?" Celeste demanded. She untangled her arms and legs from Katarina and stood up, looking down at her. "Pay attention!"

"Are either of you injured?" Madame Alla asked.

Katarina stood up and brushed herself off. "No, madame."

"That is good, but you must pay more attention, Katarina," Madame Alla said. "I said I wanted everyone to do four piqué turns, but you did five before the grand jetés. You are lucky neither you nor Celeste was hurt. You will stay behind and see me after class."

When class was over, the other dancers began to gather their things and leave. Katarina

could have sworn Celeste was smirking as she brushed by her and out the door. Sunny gave Katarina's hand a squeeze.

"I'll wait for you outside," she said softly.

Katarina nodded. Her heart was hammering in her ears. She turned around, expecting to find Madame Alla still in the dance studio, but the room was empty except for the little brown dog sleeping beside the piano.

"Lapochka!" Madame Alla called. Her voice came from the direction of her office, which was just off the dance studio. At the sound of his name, the tiny dog jumped up and trotted into the office. And then Madame Alla said, "Katarina!"

With a little less enthusiasm than the dog, Katarina walked to Madame Alla's office. It felt like she was wearing lead shoes, and it took every bit of effort she had to take each step.

She found Madame Alla sitting in a chair behind a desk in the small office, dunking a tea bag into a delicate china teacup. The woman gestured for Katarina to sit in the chair opposite her. Katarina waited, hardly able to breathe, as Madame Alla squeezed the tea bag with a spoon, blew across the top of the liquid, and took a slow sip.

"So, Katarina," she finally said. "You are a very promising dancer."

Katarina blinked. That wasn't what she'd been expecting. She'd come in here expecting to be in trouble, not to be praised.

"I . . . I am?" she said.

Madame Alla nodded. "You have wonderful musicality and expressiveness when you dance. These are gifts that cannot be taught. It makes people *want* to watch you."

Katarina was stunned. "Thank you."

Madame Alla arched an eyebrow at her. "But!"

"But?" Katarina echoed with a cringe.

"*But* you will never be a truly great ballet

dancer unless you apply yourself," she said. "I am happy that you have fun in class, because having a passion and joy for dance is essential to being a great dancer. But ballet is not *just* about passion. Ballet is also about hard work and discipline."

Katarina nodded. She knew Madame Alla was right. "Yes, madame."

"You still have much to learn about ballet technique," Madame Alla continued, "and you will not learn it if you are . . . what is the term? 'Gooping off'?"

Katarina frowned. "Do you mean 'goofing off'?"

"Ah, yes," Madame Alla said. "You will not learn if you are *goofing off* with Sunny during class. You could be a great dancer, Katarina, but you must work for it. Is that something you are willing to do?"

"Oh, yes, madame!" Katarina said. "I really do want to keep learning and getting better. I promise I'll work harder."

"Very good," Madame Alla said, giving Katarina one of her rare smiles. "Now, off you go, and I will see you next week."

Katarina thanked her and gave Lapochka a quick pet on her way out the door. She found Sunny waiting her for on the sidewalk just outside the studio.

"What did she say?" Sunny asked. "Was she mad?"

Katarina shook her head. "She just told me I need to work harder and stop gooping off with you if I want to be a great dancer."

". . . gooping?" Sunny repeated.

Katarina smiled and shrugged her shoulders. "That's what she said! Now let's get going. I don't want my dad to worry."

After the subway ride home with Sunny, Katarina walked the few blocks back to her apartment building, waved at the orange cat in the window across the street, and entered her building. As she climbed the third set of stairs up to her floor, she could hear her dad talking to someone on the other side of their door. The walls in their building were so thin that sometimes she could even hear Mr. Epstein next door, who got terrible hay fever in the summer, sneeze.

"I know," her dad was saying. "I just need a small loan to tide me over. Money's been really tight lately, and the bills are piling up."

Katarina froze as she was lifting her key to the lock.

"Things haven't been great at work," he was saying. "My commissions are way down and . . . No, I can't do that. Katarina loves those classes."

Katarina felt like someone had punched her in the gut. She hadn't realized her dad was struggling with money so much. And still he was paying for her ballet classes, even though she knew they must be expensive.

Katarina opened the door and stepped into the apartment.

"I've got to go," her dad said into the phone, quickly hanging it up. "Hey, honey! How was ballet?"

"It was good," she said. He was sitting at his computer, piles of papers around him. Bills, probably. He closed his laptop and quickly gathered the papers, shoving them into his briefcase.

He didn't want her to know about their money troubles. Probably didn't want her to feel guilty about the cost of her ballet classes.

She went up to him and gave him a huge hug.

"Hey," he said, rubbing his hands across her back. "What's this for?"

"Nothing," she said. "Just for being the best dad in the world."

"Superdad!" he said in his silly superhero voice.

That was it. No more goofing around in ballet class, not when her dad was sacrificing so much so that she could take them. She was going to make it worth his while by working hard and becoming the best ballet dancer she could possibly be.

Chapter 7

*T*HAT FRIDAY KATARINA met Sunny after school with her pajamas and clothes for the next day packed into her backpack. The Kapoors took them to a movie theater near their house, and Katarina and Sunny sat in the balcony with their popcorn and Milk Duds to watch *Leap!* It was about a girl who dreams of becoming a ballerina and gets to audition for the Paris Opera Ballet. It was Sunny's favorite movie because there was lots and lots of dancing in it. But Katarina could barely pay attention. She kept thinking about the worry in her dad's voice and the stack of bills he had tried to hide from her.

"Hey, are you okay?" Sunny asked as they walked back to her house after the movie was over. "You've been really quiet."

"We were in a movie theater," Katarina said. "You're *supposed* to be quiet."

Sunny smiled and rolled her eyes. "You know what I mean. Is everything all right?"

Katarina sighed. "Actually, I am pretty worried about something. I overheard my dad on the phone last night, and he's having trouble paying our bills. I guess he's not making as much at work as he usually does, and with the new cost of my ballet classes . . ."

"Oh, I see." Sunny frowned. "That's a tough one. But I bet we can figure something out! We've got all night tonight and all day tomorrow to think about it."

They thought about it, but Katarina and

Sunny didn't come up with any solutions as they played Just Dance on the Wii, ate dinner, and gave each other funny hairstyles. It was only when they were lying in their sleeping bags on Sunny's floor, the lights out and Sunny's cat, Milo, snoring peacefully between them, that Sunny suddenly sat up.

"I've got it!" she said.

Katarina's eyes flew open. "Yeah?"

"Yeah!" Sunny turned on her desk lamp, which gave the room a warm glow. "We take the train all the time with Beatz, right?"

"Right."

"And he plays his music for donations from people riding the train," Sunny said. "We could do the same thing with our dancing!"

"Dance on the train?" Katarina said. "Wouldn't we just fall over anytime the train takes a curve?"

Sunny laughed. "We don't have to do it on the train. We'll go somewhere where people appreciate ballet, and we'll dance for whoever is walking by. That way you can practice your technique *and* we can make some money to pay for your lessons at the same time!"

"Oh my gosh, Sunny, you're a *genius*!" Katarina said. This plan could solve her two biggest problems all at once!

Sunny's grin was huge. "I know, right?"

"We'd better get to sleep," Katarina said, snuggling down into her sleeping bag. "We've got a long day of dancing coming up tomorrow!"

The next morning they asked Mrs. Kapoor if she would take them to Lincoln Center. They'd decided that was the perfect place to try out their plan since both the New York City Ballet and the American Ballet Theatre performed there, so there were bound to be ballet lovers around. Mrs. Kapoor agreed, and because the girls' original plan for that day had been to go to the park with Lulu, they picked her up first.

"Okay, girls," Mrs. Kapoor said when they

reached Lincoln Center. "I'm going to go to that coffee shop on the corner to work while you do your thing. Have fun!"

Katarina and Sunny decided the best place for them to perform would be in front of the big fountain in the plaza. Sunny had brought a small speaker that hooked up to her phone, and she put some classical music on. Katarina had found an old bowler hat Sunny had once worn for a tap dance recital and placed it on the ground in front of them, dropping a few coins in to get them started.

"Keep an eye on our hat, girl," she said to Lulu. Lulu lay down beside it and curled up.

"Ready?" Sunny said.

Katarina nodded. "Let's do this."

They started dancing the combination Madame Alla had been teaching them in their class. At first no one was really watching, so Sunny took the chance to give Katarina some pointers on her technique.

"You need to turn out more," Sunny said, pointing at Katarina's toes. Sunny's feet made a perfectly straight line while Katarina's looked more like a V.

"Ugh, I can't," Katarina said, glaring down at her turned-in toes. "My toes have always looked like this."

"That's okay," Sunny said. "Turnout really comes from your legs, anyway. Your feet might not ever look like mine, but you have better extension and balance than me."

"Okay, I'll work on it," Katarina said, focusing on opening up. It was a weird feeling, but she was determined to do whatever she could to improve as a dancer.

Soon the girls had gathered a small audience around them, so they focused on just doing the best performance they could. Katarina didn't feel any of the nervousness she had felt when she'd danced in front of everyone at the talent show. She thought it was probably because she had Sunny at her side. As they performed their pirouettes, pas de bourrées, and jetés, loose change and even the occasional bill rained down into the bowler hat in front of them. Lulu barked appreciatively at each donation.

When the dance was over, their little audience applauded and moved on. All except for one young woman dressed in black who came up to them after everyone else was gone.

"So, you girls like ballet, huh?" she asked.

"We love it," Katarina replied. "We take lessons at Ballet Academy East."

"Have you ever seen the New York City Ballet perform? You know they do their shows right over there," she said, pointing at one of the buildings that faced the fountain.

"I have!" Sunny replied. "My parents take me to see *The Nutcracker* there every Christmas."

"I haven't, but I would love to someday," Katarina said. The closest she'd ever gotten was watching them perform on the big screen in the Electro-Land window.

"Well, how would you like to see them today?" she asked. "My name is Molly. I'm an usher there, and I could get you in to watch the matinee performance."

Katarina's mouth dropped open, and she looked over at Sunny, who had the same expression of shock on her face. Was this girl a theater usher or her fairy godmother?

"Are you serious?" Katarina asked.

"Totally," she said.

"Oh my stars!" Sunny shrieked in joy, and the two girls hugged each other, jumping up and down. Then Sunny turned to the usher and threw herself into her arms, hugging her, too. "I love you!"

Katarina laughed at the girl's shocked expression and the way she awkwardly patted Sunny on the back. "Sure. My pleasure."

She told them where to meet her before the

performance started, and Katarina and Sunny ran to the café on the corner where Mrs. Kapoor was working on her laptop. Out of breath and speaking at the same time, they told her what had happened. It took her a minute to understand what they were saying, but once she did, she said she'd call her friend who lived nearby and go to a long lunch with Lulu while the girls went to watch the ballet.

While they were waiting to go meet Molly, Katarina and Sunny counted the money they'd collected from passersby as they danced.

"Wow, we made almost twenty-five dollars!" Sunny said when she was done totaling it up.

"That's amazing!" Katarina replied. She didn't know how much her ballet lessons actually cost, but twenty-five dollars would *have* to help. She got her cell phone out of her bag to call her dad.

"Hey, sweetie," her dad said when he

answered the phone. "What's up?"

"I just wanted to let you know I'm going to be home a little late," Katarina said. She explained to him how she and Sunny were going to see the ballet that afternoon.

"That's fantastic!" he said. "I hope you girls have a great time. I'll keep an eye on my phone in case you need me."

"I will." She took a deep breath. "I also wanted to tell you that I know my dance lessons are expensive, so I'm going to be working really hard from now on to make sure it's worth it. And I want to help pay for them. Sunny and I made almost twenty-five dollars dancing today."

Katarina's dad was silent on the other end for a second, and then he said, "Oh, honey, you don't have to do that. Boring things like worrying about money are *my* job. I just want you to have fun and learn, okay?"

"But—"

"No, don't argue with me," he said. "You love

ballet, and that's all that matters to me. Got it?"

Katarina smiled. "Got it."

"Now, take that twenty-five dollars and put it into your piggy bank or buy a T-shirt at the ballet or something," he said.

"I *did* see some really cool T-shirts in the window."

He laughed. "That's my girl. I'm the luckiest dad in the world."

"I'm the luckiest daughter," she said. "See you later?"

"You bet."

Five minutes before the show was supposed to start, Katarina and Sunny went to wait in the spot by a side door where Molly had told them to meet her. She brought them inside as the last stragglers were heading to their seats in the auditorium.

"Just act like you belong," she whispered to them as they walked.

"Tickets, ladies," another usher said as they

walked through the doors to the theater.

"It's okay. They're with me," Molly replied. Katarina held her breath, waiting for the other usher to demand their tickets and then throw them out, but he just shrugged and let Molly lead them inside. The theater was so much bigger than it had seemed from the outside. Row after row of red velvet seats faced the stage, and balconies rimmed in gold seemed to reach up practically to the sky. A chandelier that looked like a cross between the sun and a disco ball twinkled above them. The New York City Ballet theater had been designed to look like a jewelry box, Molly explained. It was the most beautiful place Katarina had ever seen. She couldn't imagine what it must be like to be one of the ballerinas who got to perform in this gorgeous theater.

"Okay, here you go," Molly said, pointing to a couple of empty seats on an aisle. "Enjoy the show, girls!"

"Thank you so much!" Katarina said as she sat. "Oh, what's the ballet today?"

"*Swan Lake.*"

"Ooh, that's one of my favorites," Sunny whispered to her as the lights started to go down. "You're going to love it."

Katarina felt like her whole body was

humming with excitement as the orchestra began to play. She'd never seen a live ballet before! She watched, enraptured, as the huge gold curtain rose to reveal the corps de ballet in old-timey costumes enjoying a party. It was the prince's birthday, and soon he would have to pick a bride. But he'd rather go out hunting with his friends, and that's where he stumbled onto the lake where he encountered the beautiful Swan Queen, Odette.

"That's Odette," Sunny whispered. "The Swan Queen."

Odette and the prince danced together and began to fall in love. The other swan maidens joined in, and at one point four of them linked hands and began to dance.

"Oh!" Katarina said softly, unable to hold the sound back. She knew this part! She recognized these steps and the ballerinas with feathers in their hair from the video she'd watched at Electro-Land. *Swan Lake* was her favorite ballet and she hadn't even known it! Now that she'd learned more about ballet, she was able to appreciate what they were doing so much more than she ever had before. She knew now how difficult all those moves were, but the dancers on the stage made them look so effortless, like their bodies were made to do those things. She thought about what Madame Alla had said: Ballet was about passion but also hard work. She'd have to work very hard if she ever wanted to be as good a dancer as the four little swans.

When the ballet was over, Katarina and Sunny jumped to their feet, clapping wildly.

"Did you like it?" Sunny asked over the roar of the crowd as the ballerina who had portrayed Odette (the Swan Queen) and Odile bowed.

Katarina's hands were starting to hurt from clapping so loudly, but she didn't care. "I *loved* it! She was amazing, wasn't she?"

Someone suddenly touched Katarina's shoulder, and she jumped. Had they been caught? Were they going to be dragged off to theater jail?

But luckily it was just Molly. "Hey, girls," she said. "Come with me."

While the rest of the audience continued to applaud as the dancers took their second bows, Katarina and Sunny snuck out of the auditorium with Molly.

"I've got one more surprise for you," she told them. She took them through a door that said STAFF ONLY and led to a long corridor. Katarina and Sunny exchanged puzzled looks as they followed. Where was Molly taking them?

At the end of the hallway and around a corner was an elevator, which they rode down one level. When the elevator doors opened, Katarina gaped at what she saw.

It was a hallway a lot like the one at school,

except this one was filled with ballet dancers. Some were taking off pieces of their costumes or walking around barefoot with their pointe shoes in their hands. All of them were sweaty. As the girls followed Molly past open doors, Katarina saw dancers removing their makeup. They had to step around a rack of feathery tutus like the ones the swan maidens had worn, and someone carrying a violin almost bumped into them.

"Do you realize where we are?" Sunny asked her quietly.

Katarina nodded. She almost didn't want to say the words, too afraid this was a dream that she'd wake up from. "We're . . . we're backstage!"

Molly stopped at a closed door and knocked lightly.

"Come in!" a voice called from inside.

"Hey, Tiler," Molly said as she opened the

door. "These are the girls I was telling you about."

"Hi, girls!" Tiler Peck, the Swan Queen herself, said as they stepped into her dressing room. "I hear you like ballet?"

Chapter 8

KATARINA COULDN'T TALK or even *think* about anything besides her visit to the ballet for days afterward.

"It was incredible!" she said to Beatz as the 7 train rumbled down the tracks toward Manhattan. "Tiler Peck is a huge star, but she let Sunny and me hang out with her in her dressing room and ask her all kinds of questions about dance and what it's like to be a professional ballerina. She was so, *so* nice!"

"That's awesome!" Beatz said, kicking his

foot so that one of his cymbals clanged in celebration.

Sunny nodded. "Yeah! She even asked us if we would do some steps for her. After we danced, she said we were both really good and had a lot of potential and should stick with it."

Katarina sighed, remembering the way Tiler had hugged her and wished her luck with her dancing. "It was the best day of my whole life."

"Other than the day you met me, right?" Beatz teased, elbowing her in the ribs.

Katarina laughed. "Well, *obviously.*"

They waved goodbye to Beatz when the train pulled into their station, then headed to the dance studio. While most of the dancers spent the minutes before class chatting with one another and "gooping" around, Katarina didn't waste any time. Ever since her conversation with Madame Alla, she'd been doing her best to stay completely focused on ballet whenever she was in the studio. So while Sunny and the others joked around, she stretched her muscles and then stood at the barre, working on her turnout. If she wanted to dance as beautifully as Tiler Peck someday, she was going to have to work hard for it!

Madame Alla, followed by Lapochka as always, came into the studio a few minutes later. The last stragglers took their places at the barre and everyone quieted down, waiting for her to clap and yell, "Music!" to Mr. Simeone for the start of their warm-up.

But instead Madame Alla said, "I have something very exciting to tell you all. Please, gather around."

All of the dancers stepped away from the barre. Madame Alla sat in the chair in front of the mirror—which was always there, but Katarina had never seen her sit in it—and they sat on the floor in a semicircle around her.

"We have been invited to participate in a very exciting event," she told them. "The School of American Ballet is starting a new ballet camp near Washington, DC, this summer. They will be inviting dancers from all over the world to come for two weeks to participate in the camp and learn from the best teachers the ballet world has to offer."

Katarina met Sunny's eye, and she looked as excited as Katarina felt. Imagine spending two whole weeks doing nothing but learning ballet from famous teachers and hanging out with dancers from other countries!

"In order to choose the dancers who will be invited to attend the camp," Madame Alla continued, "they are holding a series of competitions in cities across the world. One, the Youth America Grand Prix, will be right here in New York City next month, and you all have the chance to participate!"

The class exploded into gasps and applause and whoops of excitement. Katarina clasped Sunny's hand, and across the circle she saw

Celeste's face, which was normally in a perma-frown when she wasn't dancing, light up.

"You will have to work very hard if you want to win a spot," Madame Alla told them. "There is another dance academy that will be a part of the competition, and only two dancers in total will be chosen to attend the camp. It will be difficult, but I have great belief in you. If you want to take part in the competition, speak to me after class. Now, time to warm up!"

Katarina's mind was racing as she went through the now-familiar exercises of Madame Alla's warm-up. She wanted to go to that camp more than she'd ever wanted anything in the whole world. But she was so new to ballet dancing. She'd been working hard lately, but she still had a long way to go to catch up with her classmates when it came to knowledge and technique, not to mention her pesky pigeon toes. How could she possibly hope to win one of just two spots that dozens of dancers would be competing for? Plus, Celeste was practically a lock for one of the spots, which really meant there was only *one* up for grabs.

Well, she was just going to have to work as hard as she could to give herself the best chance possible. Katarina concentrated extra hard during class, trying to leap a little higher, hold her back a little straighter, point her toes a little more.

"Pretty cool about the competition, huh?" Sunny said as they were packing up after class was over. "Man, I would love to win a spot in that ballet camp."

"Me too," Katarina said. Even thinking about it filled her with longing. "So, you're going to sign up to compete?"

"Definitely!" Sunny said. Then her eyes widened. "Hey, what if we signed up together? We could dance a pas de deux!"

"Ooh, that's a good idea!" Katarina said. "Pas de deux," which meant "step of two" in French, was the ballet term for when two people danced together. Usually it was a man and a woman—like when Tiler Peck as Odette had danced with the man playing the prince in *Swan Lake* or when Romeo danced with Juliet—but it didn't have to be. If she and Sunny danced together, it would surely be more fun. The competition would feel more like that day the two of them had danced for people outside of Lincoln Center and less like the anxious disaster that had been her performance at her school's talent show. And with Sunny dancing there beside her, maybe no one would notice her turned-in toes! "Do you think Madame Alla would let us?"

Sunny shrugged. "No way to be sure except to ask her."

The two of them joined the group of dancers who had crowded around Madame Alla to sign up for the competition. When it was their turn, they asked if they could dance together and she said they could.

"This is going to be great!" Sunny said as they walked toward the subway. "We have the perfect excuse to hang out every day now."

"And you can keep helping me with my technique!" Katarina said.

"Absolutely! We're going to have such a good time."

"Well, we're not *just* going to have a good time, right?" Katarina said. She loved how silly and fun-loving Sunny was, but she was determined to keep taking her ballet seriously after everything that had happened. "We're also going to have to work really hard if we want any shot at getting into that ballet camp."

Sunny waved her hand, as though batting away all of Katarina's concerns. "Oh, yeah, totally."

Katarina felt a little uneasy with her friend's response, but she pushed that aside. This was going to be great.

Sunny came over to Katarina's apartment the very next afternoon to start working on their pas de deux. They pushed the living room furniture against the walls and even moved her dad's favorite chair, which Lulu was napping on, into the kitchen so that they'd have a big enough clear space to dance in.

"So, what kind of dance do you want to do?" Sunny asked as they stretched their legs, getting ready to work.

Katarina had been thinking about it all day and had nothing to show for it. "I don't know. How are we even supposed to start?"

"Good question," Sunny said. "Well, what's a dance you love?"

That was one question Katarina *didn't* have to think about. One dance immediately popped into her mind.

"That's easy! The 'Dance of the Little Swans,'" she said. Ever since the moment she'd seen the dance through the window at Electro-Land, she'd been in love. The way the ballerinas in their tutus and feathers moved in such perfect unison, like they were a single dancer instead of four separate people, was mesmerizing. And then seeing it live at the New York City Ballet had only made her love it even more.

"Okay!" Sunny said, standing. "We'll start there, then. What do you love about that dance?"

"I love how energetic it is," Katarina said. "There's so much intricate footwork, and the dancers are so light on their feet. But at the same time, it's also very difficult and delicate. Like they're floating."

Sunny tapped her fingers against her chin. "Hmm, difficult but delicate. That's a tough balance, but I bet we can do it! What if we start like this?" Sunny stood beside her and held her hand, linking their fingers together. "Now, let's do three chassés to the right."

Together they did the skipping step three

times until they ran out of room. It felt just right, full of energy but also light and graceful.

"I like it!" Katarina said. "Now, how about we let go and do a tombé pas de bourrée and then meet up again?"

"Yes!" Sunny said.

They worked this way for hours, suggesting steps to each other and trying them. Sometimes the step felt right and they kept it. Other times the step didn't quite seem to fit, so they tried something else. Eventually Lulu got up from her nap and ran around between their feet, like she was trying to join in.

"Lu, be careful," Katarina said when she almost tripped over the dog.

"I think she wants us to make this a pas de trois!" Sunny said, which was the term for a dance with three people in it.

Katarina laughed. "If we danced with a cute dog, we'd win the competition for sure."

"Lapochka would *definitely* vote for us,"

Sunny said. "There aren't nearly enough dogs in ballet."

Lulu barked her agreement, and the girls laughed and continued to work on their dance. The judges weren't going to know what hit them!

Chapter 9

"KATARINA, TIME TO wake up!" her dad said, poking his head into her room. "Breakfast is almost ready."

"Coming," she said, climbing out of bed. Her muscles cried out at the movement. "Ughh . . ." She groaned.

"Sore?" her dad asked.

She and Sunny had been getting together almost every day to work on their pas de deux, and most mornings she felt like one big ache.

"It feels like someone squeezed me through

the pasta roller you use to make linguine," she said.

He laughed. "Well, just think of it this way: Soreness is your body's way of letting you know you're getting stronger and using the correct muscles."

That did make her feel a little better. She hobbled to the table for oatmeal and fruit, and by the time she left for school, she felt almost normal again.

"How's ballet going?" Amelie asked during art class as they all worked on their paintings.

"Good," Katarina said. "I've been really working hard, and I think it's starting to pay off."

Grant frowned down at his painting, which looked more like a hedgehog than the vase of flowers they were supposed to be painting. "So, when do we get to see you dance?" he asked.

"Well, we have a competition coming up in a couple of weeks," she said. "The winners get to go to this really cool international ballet camp this summer. Would you guys want to come and watch?"

"Of course!" Michael replied. Somehow he'd gotten a dot of green paint on the tip of his nose. "We wouldn't miss it."

When the final bell rang at the end of the day, Katarina waved goodbye to her friends and rushed out of the school. Lulu was waiting for her by the fence like always, and she started to turn left toward home.

"Not that way, girl," Katarina said. "We're going to the subway."

Lulu looked confused, but she dutifully followed Katarina in the opposite direction of home, toward the subway station. Usually on the days Katarina had ballet class, she went back to her apartment after school to have a snack and do her homework before catching the train to Manhattan with Sunny. But last night she'd emailed Madame Alla to ask if she could come in early to practice in the dance studio. She could dance better with the wide-open space and the mirror so she could see what she was doing, and there was less chance of her almost breaking another lamp if she lost control of a turn.

When the 7 train pulled into the station, Katarina listened for the sound of music. She heard the bang of Beatz's drum and made sure she and Lulu got into that car. She might not have Sunny to ride with today, but at least she could see her other friend.

"Hey, Katarina Ballerina!" Beatz said, continuing to strum a melody on his guitar and bang his cymbals and drums. "I wasn't expecting to see you yet!"

"Lulu and I are going to the studio early so I can get some extra practice in," Katarina explained, taking a seat on the bench near Beatz.

"Good for you," he said. "Real artists put the time in. When I was your age, I used to play my guitar for so many hours that my fingers would sometimes start to bleed."

"Wow, really?"

"Yep, that's how I got all these calluses," he said, showing her his hands. The tips of his fingers were rough with thick skin. "All good guitarists have them. It means you're working hard."

"I'm starting to get stronger!" Katarina said. "At first my feet were tired after class from being in ballet slippers, but now I feel like I can just keep on going."

Beatz nodded. "Same thing."

When the subway reached her stop, Katarina said goodbye to Beatz and headed for the ballet studio. Madame Alla let her in.

"Thanks again for letting me come in early," Katarina said.

"It is my pleasure," the teacher said. "I'm happy you're putting so much effort into your dancing."

"Is it okay if Lulu comes in too?" Katarina said, gesturing to the dog at her feet. "She'll be good, I promise."

Just then Lapochka came running into the room. He strutted up to Lulu and sniffed around her, then touched his nose to hers. The two of them began to romp around the room, chasing each other and pretending to wrestle.

"It looks like she and Lapochka are best friends already," Madame Alla said. "I will be in my office. Let me know if you need anything."

"Thank you, Madame Alla."

Katarina stretched while the two little dogs chased each other. By the time she was warmed up and ready to start dancing, Lulu and Lapochka had worn each other out and were sleeping side by side next to the piano. Katarina worked on her dance moves alone until the other dancers in her class started to arrive. She worked on her turnout so she could get her feet into proper fifth position. Katarina lifted her leg to the back to work on her arabesque with a nice, straight leg and pointed toe. And she tried to perfect her port de bras, moving her arms up and over her head gracefully like the dancers on the TV at Electro-Land—and just like she imagined her mom had done when she'd danced.

Over the last couple of weeks, her technique had really improved and she didn't stick out like a sore thumb in class anymore. She could do all the steps the other dancers could do and almost as well. Her bun might not be as smooth and her turned-in toes might not look quite right, but she was getting a little better every day. All of her hard work was paying off.

After class, she went up to the ballet teacher. "Madame Alla, would it be okay if I came in to do some extra practice more often?" she asked.

"Of course. Any time, Katarina." She winked. "Lapochka would appreciate the company."

"Thank you, madame!" Katarina said. She and Sunny headed for the subway to return home. "Hey, you should come in with me next time. It would be great to rehearse our pas de deux in front of the mirrors so we can see if there's anything that needs to be fixed."

"Sure!" Sunny said.

They agreed to meet at the dance studio after school on Thursday, but their meeting time came and went and Sunny wasn't there. Katarina stretched and began to practice on her own. Eventually, fifteen minutes after they were supposed to start practicing, Sunny came running through the door.

"Sorry!" she said. "I was talking to my friend Alice after school, and I totally lost track of the time."

Katarina tried to push away her annoyance. It wasn't like Sunny had been late on purpose, after all. It was an honest mistake. "That's okay. Let's get working."

"Sure, but first I have to show you this hilarious picture I took of Milo this morning," Sunny said, digging her phone out of her bag. "He fell asleep curled up *in* my mom's house planter."

Katarina sighed but looked at the picture. It *was* pretty funny, but she was ready to get to work.

"Okay, ready?" Katarina said.

She turned on the piece of music they'd chosen to dance to, and she and Sunny took their opening positions. When the notes began to play, they started to dance. Chassé right, chassé right, chassé right, tombé pas de bourrée, arabesque, and soutenu to the left.

So far, so good. Then it was a chaîné turn upstage, clasp hands, chassé to the left. Then Sunny hit a pose as Katarina did a double-pirouette turn and landed in fourth. Then it was Sunny's turn. Katarina held her tendu back pose while Sunny was supposed to do a grand jeté and arabesque. But Sunny just stood there, wide-eyed.

"Wait, what am I supposed to be doing?" she asked.

How could Sunny not remember? Had she

not been practicing? "Jeté and arabesque!" Katarina said, annoyed.

"Oh, right!" Sunny laughed at her forgetfulness and started to perform the steps, but the music had already moved on.

"Just keep going!" Katarina said, giving Sunny a light push toward stage right where they were supposed to be by now. Sunny wasn't expecting it and almost tripped, which only made her laugh more.

"Easy, Katarina!" she said.

But Katarina could feel her face getting hot. "Stop playing around!" she snapped.

Sunny finally seemed to realize how angry Katarina was, and she stopped dancing. "What's your problem?"

"You're goofing off, and I'm trying to work," Katarina said. "I want to win this competition and I can only do that if we take it seriously!"

"You're taking it *too* seriously," Sunny said. "We've been rehearsing almost every day! The

world's not going to end if I laugh or forget a step every once in a while."

"But we don't have much time until the competition, so we have to use every minute we get," Katarina said. "I want to be a great dancer someday, and that means I have to work hard."

Sunny threw up her hands. "But ballet's supposed to be *fun*, remember? Isn't that why you wanted to do it in the first place?"

"It's not *just* supposed to be fun, though!" Katarina said.

Sunny stalked to the wall and grabbed her bag. "Well, right now it's not *any* fun, so I don't want to do this anymore."

"Fine!" Katarina said. "Maybe I'll be better off without you!"

"Fine!" Sunny retorted as she stormed out of the studio, leaving Katarina all alone.

Chapter 10

AFTER HER FIGHT with Sunny, Katarina couldn't concentrate on dancing anymore. Her limbs seemed as heavy as lead, and the idea of trying to do a turn or a leap was suddenly exhausting. She gave up, and packed her things.

"Come on, Lulu," she said. The little dog trotted up to her and gave her a lick on the cheek. "Let's get out of here, girl."

Katarina meant to get on the train home, but instead of riding west toward Queens, she found herself heading uptown. She emerged from the subway station in front of Lincoln Center just as the sun was beginning to go down and the windows of the theater where she and Sunny had watched *Swan Lake* were glinting orange. She walked to the spot where she and Sunny had danced that afternoon. A bunch of pigeons were milling around, pecking at invisible crumbs, and she swore it felt like they were mocking her with their turned-in toes.

No great ballerinas have turned-in toes, she seemed to hear them say as they cooed. *You'll never be a great dancer no matter how hard you work.*

"Shoo!" Katarina said, scattering the birds. The backs of her eyes were stinging with unshed tears as she sat down on the paving stones where she and Sunny had danced together what felt like a lifetime ago. Dancing here that day and seeing her first live ballet had probably been the best day of her life, so how had she ended up here now, miserable and all by herself?

Lulu curled up beside her, pushing her wet nose into Katarina's hand to be petted.

"Okay," Katarina said with a small smile, scratching Lulu's ears. "Not *all* by myself."

Maybe Sunny was right. Maybe in her determination to become a better dancer, Katarina had lost sight of why she loved ballet in the first place. She loved the beauty of it. And it was a big connection to her mom.

But Katarina bet that her mom danced because of how it made her feel. Katarina was always worrying so much about her toes and her technique that she hadn't had *fun* dancing in a long time, maybe since the day she and Sunny had danced right here in this plaza. If she worked her tail off and became the world's best ballerina but she didn't enjoy it anymore, then what was the point?

Just then Katarina heard the tapping of shoes against the paving stones, and she looked up to see a woman walking straight for her, her eyes down on her phone.

"Watch out!" Katarina said, scrambling to her feet.

"Oh!" The woman jumped back. "I'm sorry. I didn't see you there!"

It was Tiler Peck. Katarina tried to speak, but no words came out of her mouth. Somehow seeing one of the world's best ballerinas walking around on the street like a normal person was even more amazing than seeing her backstage at the ballet had been.

Tiler cocked her head at Katarina. "Hey, I know you, don't I?"

Katarina swallowed and forced herself to speak. "I—I'm Katarina."

"Oh, right!" Tiler said. "You're one of the budding ballerinas I met after the show a couple of weeks ago. Is your friend here too?"

Katarina shook her head, feeling the tears build behind her eyes again. She wasn't sure if Sunny even *was* her friend anymore. "No."

"Hey, are you okay?" Tiler asked, touching her arm. When Katarina didn't know how to answer her, Tiler continued. "Tell you what. I was just headed to this café down the street that makes the best hot chocolate. I like to get one after I've had a hard day. It always makes me feel better. How about you come with me and we'll both get one?"

Katarina nodded, and she and Lulu followed Tiler to the nearby café. Tiler was so kind and friendly as they ordered their hot chocolates and sat down at a small table in the corner that Katarina's nervousness from being around the ballet star began to melt away. When Tiler asked what had her down, the whole story spilled out of Katarina like she was talking to one of her best friends. She told Tiler all about the dance competition that was coming up,

her fight with Sunny, and how hard she'd been working at becoming a better dancer.

"Sunny said I'm working so hard that I've forgotten ballet is supposed to be *fun*," she told Tiler, "and I'm starting to think she might be right. I'm just . . . well, I guess I'm scared."

"Of what?" Tiler asked.

Katarina shrugged. "A lot of things, like the money my dad is spending on my lessons. Or that the pigeons are right and no matter how hard I work to make my technique better, I'll never fit in as a dancer anyway because of my stupid toes."

Tiler arched an eyebrow. "Pigeons talk to you?"

"Not really. I just imagine they do sometimes."

"Okay, good, because that would be a *real* problem," Tiler said with a grin. "Now, what about these toes? Show me."

Katarina stood up and showed her how her toes turned in. "See? I'll never fit in."

"So what?" Tiler said. "Maybe you're not *supposed* to fit in!"

Katarina dropped back into her chair. "What?"

"Lots of great dancers had something a little different about them," Tiler said. "Sometimes the things that make us different are also what make us special."

"You think so?" Katarina said. "But what about my turnout? With toes like these, I'll never have great turnout, and Madame Alla says that's really important."

"Well, don't tell Madame Alla this," Tiler said, leaning farther over the table so that she could whisper to Katarina, "but turnout isn't everything. You know who else doesn't have great turnout?"

"Who?" Katarina whispered back.

"Me!" Tiler said.

"What? No way!"

Tiler nodded. "But if I'm doing my job right and putting all of my love and passion into my dancing so that it makes the person watching me feel something, that's what's important to me."

"You're right," Katarina said, awed.

"Plus, a little less turnout has worked in my favor. I'm able to move quickly and do intricate footwork, and some ballerinas who have

great turnout and more flexibility might have a harder time moving as quickly," Tiler continued. "In ballet we want to give the illusion of perfection, and that can feel like a lot to live up to. But no dancer is perfect, just like no person is perfect. So it's just about using what you have the best way you can. You don't need to be anything other than who you are."

Katarina replayed those words over and over in her mind as she walked to the subway after saying goodbye to Tiler. If she could just focus on becoming the best dancer she could be, instead of trying to become a *perfect* dancer, it would take a huge weight off her shoulders!

But she wanted a second opinion, so she was relieved when she found Beatz on the train. He was playing a lively tune, beads of sweat forming on his forehead as he jerked his drums and strummed his guitar and blew into his harmonica. Just like Tiler Peck, he made it look easy unless you looked *really* close to see how hard he was actually working.

"Hi, Beatz!" Katarina said when he finished the song.

"Katarina Ballerina," he said. "How are you this fine evening?"

"I'm okay," she replied. "Can I ask you something?"

"Of course!"

"Do you think you can be a good artist even if you're different?" Katarina asked.

"Let me ask *you* something," he said, leaning close to her. "Have you ever seen someone play an instrument like this one?"

Katarina looked at the crazy contraption strapped to Beatz's back. "No, I guess I haven't."

"Well, there's your answer!" Beatz said. "Believe it or not, I actually trained as a cellist."

Katarina gaped. She couldn't imagine Beatz in a tuxedo playing classical musical in a symphony. *"Really?"*

"Yep!" he said. "But it just wasn't me. It didn't ignite that fire in me that good art is supposed to. But this does."

"Do you think that fire is the most important thing?" Katarina asked.

"Absolutely!" Beatz said. "Now, you have to put in the dedication in order to develop the muscles you need to create art. But the fire inside of you, the passion for what you're creating, is what will make your art captivating."

"Do you think I could be a captivating dancer someday?" she asked. "If I keep training my muscles?"

"I think you're already a captivating dancer," he said. "Because you love to dance and that love radiates out of you. Technique can be learned, but passion can't, and I've seen that passion in you since the first day we met. Here, let me show you."

Beatz struck up a song, and Katarina knew what she had to do. She stood up and started to dance, but she didn't worry about the steps or how much her toes were pointed or how turned out her hips were. She just moved the way the music made her feel, the way she used to. The rumble of the train and the people around her seemed to fade away until all she was aware of was the music and the movement of her body.

When the music ended, Katarina heard applause. She opened her eyes—which she hadn't realized she had closed—and saw all the people who had stopped what they were doing to watch her dance.

"See?" Beatz whispered in her ear. "That's what the fire in you can do."

Chapter 11

KATARINA WENT TO Sunny's house to apologize, but before she could even get the words out, Sunny apologized to *her*. They hugged and promised they would do a better job of telling the other how they were feeling from then on.

Then Katarina went home and started to add to the collection of ballerina photos on her walls. She taped up pictures of the dancers who inspired her: Tiler Peck, Misty Copeland, Michaela DePrince, a soloist for the Dutch National

Ballet . . . and the most important of all: her mom.

Before Katarina knew it, it was time for the ballet competition. She and Sunny had been working hard (*and* having fun!), and she thought their pas de deux was ready. Lulu and Lapochka, at least, had seemed to enjoy watching it the last time they'd rehearsed at the studio!

The competition was being held on the New York City Ballet stage in Midtown, and Katarina felt just like one of the dancers as she and Sunny got ready in their dressing room with some of the other girls from their class. As Katarina was struggling to get her curly hair into the smoothest bun possible, she spotted Celeste in the mirror standing just outside the dressing room, cell phone held to her ear.

"But the competition starts at seven! I told you about it weeks ago," she was saying quietly into the phone. Katarina wasn't *trying* to eavesdrop, but she couldn't help herself. "Uh-huh . . . I'll try my best, but there are a lot of dancers competing, so . . . Yes, ma'am. I know—there's no point competing if you aren't going to win."

Celeste looked like she was on the verge of tears when she hung up, and Katarina felt a surge of sympathy for her. Before she'd headed backstage, her dad had given her a big hug and told her he was proud of her no matter what happened.

"Hey, are you okay?" she asked as Celeste came in.

The other girl looked down at the red leotard Katarina was wearing. She and Sunny had decided on this costume as a little tribute to the first day they met.

"What are you wearing?" she asked sharply.

But this time it didn't make Katarina feel bad, because she thought she was beginning to understand why Celeste could be such a jerk sometimes.

"Come on," Sunny said, tapping Katarina's shoulder. "Let's go get warmed up."

There was a room set aside backstage for dancers to stretch and do some last-minute practice in front of the mirror before being called out onstage to dance. Katarina and Sunny ran through the normal warm-up they did in Madame Alla's class and then began practicing some of the trickier bits of their pas de deux. They nailed every step, and Katarina was feeling more confident than she ever had before.

"This is going to be great!" she said. "I'm so glad we decided to do this together."

"Me too," Sunny said. "Maybe we could even beat Celeste and go to the ballet camp together."

"That would be amazing," Katarina said. She caught a glimpse of the clock on the wall. "Oh, the competition's about to start. We'd better go find Madame Alla."

Sunny waved to the other dancers warming up around them. "*Merde*, everyone!" she said, and most of them said it back.

"What's *'merde'*?" Katarina asked as they walked away.

"It's what dancers say before a show," Sunny told her. "In the theater, they say 'break a leg,' but dancers don't, for obvious reasons. It's French, just like everything else."

"What does it mean?" Katarina asked as they approached the short staircase that led back to the dressing rooms.

Sunny laughed. "My mom would be mad at me if I told you! It's not as bad as what they do in the opera, though. They pretend to spit on you for good luck!"

They were halfway down the stairs when Sunny's foot suddenly slipped out from under her. She lost her balance and tumbled down the last four steps, collapsing into a heap at the bottom.

"Sunny!" Katarina cried, rushing to her friend's side. "Are you okay?"

Sunny was clutching her ankle. "Ow, ow, ow, ow, ow!"

Madame Alla had heard the commotion and came running to them. She felt around Sunny's ankle with her fingers while Sunny gripped Katarina's hand.

"Is it broken?" Katarina asked.

"No, only sprained," Madame Alla announced. "You will be fine in a week or two, Sunny, but I'm afraid you will not be able to dance tonight."

Katarina felt like her stomach had dropped into her feet. "Oh no! Sunny, I'm so sorry!"

"It's okay, Katarina. Don't feel bad," Sunny said as Madame Alla helped her to stand. Katarina wrapped her arm around Sunny's waist so that her friend could lean on her. Together she and Madame Alla helped Sunny hop back to the dressing room, where she could sit down.

"I can't believe we're not going to get to dance in the competition," Katarina said. They'd worked so hard, but all of Katarina's dreams of somehow winning a place at that ballet camp had evaporated.

"No, silly, *I'm* not going to get to dance," Sunny said. "There's nothing stopping you! You'll just have to do our pas de deux by yourself."

"Oh no, I can't do that," Katarina said. "We were supposed to do this together!"

"You've worked too hard and come too far not to give it a try," Sunny said. "Please? If I'm not going to get to go to that ballet camp, then you *have* to so you can at least tell me all about it."

"She is right, Katarina," Madame Alla said. "You deserve to take your chance, and the audience deserves to see you perform."

"Really?" Katarina asked, looking back and forth between the two of them. The idea of going out on the stage by herself instead of with her friend at her side filled her stomach with butterflies. What if she froze up again, the way she had at the talent show?

"Yes!" they both said.

Katarina took a deep breath. "Okay. I'll do it."

By the time Katarina was on-deck to dance, the butterflies in her stomach had turned into great big bats. Madame Alla stood in the wings with her as she watched Celeste dance onstage. She really was a beautiful dancer; she'd get one of the spots at the ballet camp for sure.

Celeste finished dancing and bowed to

thunderous applause. Katarina couldn't believe how loud it was. How many people were out there in the audience? Madame Alla gave her shoulder a squeeze.

"You can do this, Katarina," she said. *"Merde."*

"And now our final dancers of the evening," the host onstage said. "From the Ballet Academy East, Katarina Marin and Suhanisa Kapoor!"

Katarina tried to swallow down her fear and then stepped out onto the stage. She took her opening position and heard a murmur go through the crowd in the silence before the music started when no other dancer joined her. Katarina's hand, which was supposed to be clasped with Sunny's at the beginning of their pas de deux, felt extra empty.

As the delicate strings of the violin rose, Katarina began to dance. She did the opening chassé sequence. The butterflies were still flapping around in her stomach, but she began to feel like things might be okay. She nailed her double pirouette and landed in fourth, just like they'd practiced, so that Sunny could do her grand jeté and arabesque.

But, of course, Sunny wasn't there.

Katarina didn't know what to do. For a couple of beats she just stood there, her mind racing as she tried to figure out how she'd fill in the holes in the pas de deux that Sunny's absence had left. She tried to do the jeté and arabesque herself, but now she was rattled and she wobbled so much during the arabesque that she had to put the leg she'd lifted into the air back down on the floor so she wouldn't fall. She was suddenly very aware of the rows and rows of people staring at her. This wasn't like the real "Dance of the Little Swans," where the dancers had one another to blend in with, and all of the advice Tiler had given her about celebrating the things that made her different went flying out of her head. The hundreds of eyes in the room were on her. She looked out over the crowd, trying to find the reassuring faces of her dad or her friends, but she didn't see anyone she recognized. She tried to keep dancing, but the routine didn't work right with Sunny's parts missing, and Katarina's limbs began to feel heavier and heavier as she struggled through the dance.

They're all staring at me, she thought. *They're looking at my bumpy bun and my turned-in toes!*

Katarina stopped dancing. In her panic, she couldn't remember which step came next. All she wanted to do was run off the stage.

But suddenly, from the back of the theater, she heard the sound of enthusiastic drumming.

Chapter 12

*K*ATARINA SQUINTED PAST the lights, trying to see where the mysterious drumming was coming from. But when she heard the guitar and harmonica join in, she didn't need to look anymore to know. It was Beatz!

Listening to Beatz's music—which was so him, and full of the love and passion he always put into his music—Katarina realized it didn't matter if her toes didn't look like the other dancers' or if she wobbled during her arabesque or even if she won a place in the ballet camp. What mattered was that she loved dancing and this was her chance to share that love with everyone else in this room.

Katarina grinned and took the tie out of her bun, shaking her curls loose. Like Beatz playing the cello, having a perfectly smooth ballerina bun just wasn't *her*. Her wild curls were, and she was done trying to fight them. Her curls and her turned-in toes and everything else that made her a little bit different were also what made her *special*.

Katarina started to dance along with Beatz's exuberant song, just like she'd done on the subway so many times. She moved her body however the music made her feel. Sometimes that meant ballet steps, but other times it was steps that were entirely her own. Her love for dancing burned like a flame deep in the center of her chest, and as the music transported her, she felt it spreading out, all the way to the tips of her fingers and toes, and she wondered if it had left her entirely and was now spreading to the audience around her.

As she danced, Katarina glanced into the wings, where she spotted Sunny leaning on one crutch, cheering her along. Katarina jetéd across the stage toward her, took her hand, and led her out onto the stage. Katarina danced and Sunny kind of joined in. She couldn't do any footwork, but she made graceful movements with her free arm and lifted her hurt foot behind her in the most beautiful arabesque Katarina had ever seen.

The other dancers from their class were watching from backstage too, and Katarina beckoned to them. She wanted them out there with her, not because she wanted to blend in with them or to hide from the eyes of the audience, but because she wanted to share the love she was feeling with them. They streamed out of the wings to join her, everyone moving the way Beatz's music made them feel. Even Celeste eventually came out onto the stage, and Katarina saw a huge smile spread across her face as she began to dance.

Out in the audience, someone suddenly stood up out of their seat and began to dance in the aisle. The lights in the auditorium began to come up, and Katarina realized the dancer was Tiler Peck! Farther up the aisle, Beatz was rocking his one-man band, and lots of audience members were clapping or bopping along in their chairs. Katarina spotted her dad and her school friends in the second row, and she ran down the steps on the side of the stage to go join them. Her dad jumped up and started dancing with her in the aisle, and her friends followed.

"This is so great!" her dad said over the sound of the music.

"I love ballet!" Grant added, doing a definitely non-ballet dance move that involved

him moving his arms around his head like a sprinkler.

When Katarina glanced around, she saw that many of the dancers from her class had joined her in the auditorium and most of the audience was on its feet, dancing along with them. They all danced together until Katarina's heart was practically bursting, and she was sure everyone else could feel it too.

When Beatz's song came to an end, the whole theater erupted in cheers and applause. Katarina ran up to Beatz and gave him the best hug she could around all of the instruments strapped to his body.

"Thank you!" she told him. "You really saved me."

He kissed her cheek. "Thank *you*, Katarina Ballerina."

The host stepped back out onto the stage with her microphone and a big smile. "Well, that was certainly different, wasn't it?" she said. "Let's have a hand for Katarina Marin and Suhanisa Kapoor!"

The applause was as loud as thunder in Katarina's ears.

"And a round of applause for our mysterious musician," the host continued, pointing to Beatz, "and to all of you for the excellent dancing *you* did this evening!"

Katarina heard her dad's distinctive whistle, even over all of the clapping and cheering.

"I'd like to ask all the dancers to come back out onto the stage while our judges make their final decisions," the host said. Katarina said goodbye to Beatz, and her dad and school friends waved to her as she headed to the stairs that would take her back onto the stage. Before she got there, a hand reached out and stopped her.

It was Tiler Peck. "Good luck, Katarina!" she said.

"Thanks!" Katarina breathed. The truth was,

tonight had been so amazing that she didn't care anymore if she won or not.

Katarina gathered onstage with the other dancers in Madame Alla's class to await the judges' decisions.

"You were incredible!" Sunny whispered to her as they stood side by side. "It was like you were lit up from the inside. I loved watching you, *ma belle pamplemousse*."

Katarina giggled. "Did you just call me your beautiful grapefruit?"

Sunny grinned. "Yep."

"Well, thank you," Katarina said. "I couldn't have done any of this without your help."

Celeste sidled up on her other side.

"Hey, Katarina," she said.

Katarina blinked in surprise. It was the first nice thing she could ever remember Celeste saying to her. "Oh, uh, hi, Celeste."

"I just wanted to say . . . that was the most fun I've had dancing in a long, long time," Celeste said. "You're going to have to teach me some of those moves of yours sometime."

Katarina grinned. Maybe Celeste wasn't so bad after all. "Deal."

Just then the host stepped back onto the stage with a piece of paper in her hand. She was about to announce the winners! Katarina grabbed Sunny's hand, and Sunny gave her fingers a reassuring squeeze.

"Okay, everyone, I have the judges' decision," the host said. "You all did a fantastic job tonight and should be very proud, but only two of you will win a place at the Washington Ballet Summer Intensive in Washington, DC, this summer."

Suddenly Celeste grabbed Katarina's other hand. Katarina smiled and gave her hand a squeeze to encourage Celeste the same way Sunny had her.

"And the first spot goes to . . ."—Beatz struck up a drumroll out in the audience—"Celeste Hart!"

Celeste looked like she might faint when her name was announced, and Katarina and Sunny cheered for her along with everyone in the audience. She had danced so beautifully that she definitely deserved a spot at the camp. When Celeste was too stunned to step forward to take a bow, Katarina laughed and gave her a little push.

The host lifted the microphone back to her mouth. "And the final spot at WBSI goes to . . ."

Sunny gripped Katarina's hand so hard, she thought her fingers might break. But although Katarina would dearly love to go to that dance camp, all of her nerves were suddenly gone. She'd worked hard and done her best, and she'd shared her love of dancing with everyone in that theater. She couldn't ask for anything more than that. It had been the absolute best night of her life.

"Katarina Marin!" the host announced.

Three Months Later

"**OKAY, GIRLS,**" **KATARINA'S** dad said as they arrived at the college campus in Washington, DC, where they'd be attending the dance camp for the next two weeks. "Are you ready?"

Katarina turned to Celeste, who was sitting beside her in the back seat of her dad's car.

"I guess so," Celeste said.

Katarina grinned and tucked one of her loose curls behind her ear. "Let's do this!"

They parked in front of the main building

and climbed out of the car. While her dad unloaded their suitcases, Katarina and Celeste looked around at all the other young dancers who were arriving from countries all over the world. There was going to be so much to learn here, and Katarina couldn't wait to get started! She and Celeste shouldered their dance bags and got ready to walk inside the building, which had a sign on the door that said DANCER REGISTRATION.

"Oh man, I'm really nervous," Celeste confessed.

Katarina took her friend's hand. "Just be yourself, because you're special just the way you are. Got it?"

Celeste smiled. "Got it."

Katarina took a deep breath, ready to run up the stairs and toward whatever experiences were waiting for her inside. "Here we go!"

Acknowledgments

STORYBOOKS HAVE THE incredible power to move children and shape the way they feel and interact with the world. As a little girl, Tiler remembers reading her favorite book about dance over and over again and being enchanted by the idea that dance is a universal language that has the ability to move everyone too. When Kyle was little, he took a dance class and locked himself inside a bathroom the day he found out he had to perform in the recital. To this day, he wonders what might have been if he had seen it through. We are hoping that this book will inspire kids of all ages to own what makes them unique and embrace their own special gifts. Work hard, be kind, and dream big, and you'll be amazed at what's possible!

We want to extend a special thank-you to Alyson Heller and the entire Aladdin/Simon & Schuster team—Mara Anastas, Chriscynethia Floyd, Tiara Iandiorio, Chelsea Morgan, Nicole Russo, Lauren Carr, Caitlin Sweeny, Alissa Nigro, and Anna Jarzab—for making our dreams a reality. You surrounded us with so much warmth and guidance, and we knew from our first meeting: *Katarina Ballerina* had found the dream team.

To our agent, Lacy Lynch, and to Dabney Rice of Dupree Miller, for your tireless work and support. You believed in us as authors and in our book from the very beginning, and we couldn't have done this without your guidance and passion for storytelling.

To Cristin Terrill and Sumiti Collina, thank you for hearing our voices and pouring your heart into the story and illustrations to help us bring Katarina to life.

Tiler would also like to thank Lauren Auslander and her LUNA team for being the link that made all of this possible. Your work ethic and professionalism is unmatched, but more important, you are an absolute pleasure to work with. Thank you for always pushing me to dream big and then making those dreams become realities.

Victoria Morris, for always having my best interests at heart. You have been by my side since I was eight years old, and I look forward to many more years of friendship.

Finally, to the one constant in my life: my family. Your unwavering love and support is something I feel grateful for every day. Thank you, Grandma, for your dedication to my training and encouragement to live a life beyond what you had. My mother, who was my first dance teacher and continues to teach and inspire the next generation and me. My dad, for always being the rock for us girls. And to my sister, Myka, who has been the best role model a sister could ask for. Your strength and selflessness astound me every day.

About the Authors

TILER PECK is an award-winning international ballerina and has been a principal dancer with New York City Ballet since 2009. As an actress, she has been seen on Broadway in *On The Town* (as Ivy) and *The Music Man* (as Gracie). She originated the role of Marie in the Kennedy Center's production of *Little Dancer* (now called *Marie*), which is Broadway-bound with Tiler attached to star alongside her coauthor, Kyle Harris. She is a recipient of the 2013 Princess Grace Statue Award and a 2016 *Dance Magazine* Award and was named one of the *Forbes* 30 Under 30 in Hollywood & Entertainment. Tiler was the first woman to curate three *BalletNOW* performances at the Music Center in Los Angeles, and she starred in the Hulu documentary *Ballet Now*. She is the designer of Tiler Peck Designs for Body Wrappers, a line of dancewear for all ages. She lives in New York City with her dog, Cali, but her heart splits time between the Big Apple and her small hometown in California, where she was first introduced to dance at her mom's studio.

KYLE HARRIS is a Broadway and television actor who grew up as a soccer player in Irvine, California. Kyle recently starred in the popular Freeform series *Stitchers*, has appeared in *Sondheim on Sondheim*, and is currently in the new hit play *The Inheritance* on Broadway. He toured the country as Tony in the Broadway national tour of *West Side Story* and starred opposite his coauthor, Tiler Peck, in the Broadway-bound musical *Little Dancer*. Kyle has also appeared on the TV shows *The Carrie Diaries*, *Beauty and the Beast*, *High Maintenance*, *God Friended Me*, and *The Blacklist: Redemption*. If it weren't for his mother introducing him to children's books at a young age and his grandmothers' encouragement of his creative talents, he knows he wouldn't be as well-rounded and successful in the arts as he is today.

SUMITI COLLINA is a magenta-haired illustrator based in Italy. She was born in Ravenna in 1990 and from that moment loved drawing and being a night owl. Determined not to ever live without pets, she lives with two very rustic dogs. She has illustrated stories and fairy tales for clients all around the world.

**WATCH FOR
KATARINA'S
NEXT ADVENTURE,
COMING IN 2021!**